Accidentally Yours

short works
by Joan H. Young

Table of Contents

Introduction

This collection includes a wide variety of genres and styles of writing. Although the "experts" say an anthology should be arranged around one theme or genre, my personal forté is to be diverse. Therefore, the apparent theme is that these stories, poems, and essays all came from my chaotic mind.

Most any entry will be different in tone from the previous one. If you have just had a warm fuzzy moment, prepare to be disturbed. If you were creeped out by a poem, the next story may be more hopeful. I have given a short introduction to many pieces so you will have some idea of what to expect.

Although my faith is a critical element of my makeup, I have chosen not to include poems and stories that are specifically faith-based in this anthology. I hope, sometime in the future, to gather a collection of those writings and present it separately.

These offerings are accidentally yours. Skip the ones you don't like and savor the ones you do.

Joan H. Young
December 2019

Accidentally Yours

FLASH FICTION — This story was originally written as an entry in a contest that was required to use a particular sentence. The story survives, but that specific sentence had to go.

The old man in the shiny suit insisted that the North Sea had also frozen in 1947. He was too loud, of course, and slightly drunk, but then, everyone was. Everyone except Havet. She sat quietly, holding a wine glass, but only taking an occasional sip. A soft white blanket was tucked around her lower body. Above the blanket could be seen a shimmering blue-green strapless gown that fitted Havet's slim body perfectly. Its iridescence sent shimmers of purple and pink, even yellow, skittering around the room whenever the light caught a fold. She was well aware that the smooth curve of her bare shoulders made James think of wind-contoured beaches, and summer sun. Waves of long blond hair swirled over those shoulders, caressing them. And she knew James longed for the end of this boring party, ached to touch those shoulders again, to comb his fingers through her hair and brush his lips against her neck. Her eyes, blue as sea ice, followed him, reading his thoughts. She smiled—their secret was safe with her.

One flaw marred Havet's lovely skin. What appeared to be a dimple in her upper left arm was, instead, a cruel scar. The wound had been carefully repaired by a highly-skilled plastic surgeon, and when she tucked her hair behind a shell-like ear, a matching scar on the underarm was revealed. The indentations were still an angry red, although nearly healed. A small amount of makeup helped mask the dark reminders of the horrible accident.

James came to her side and bent to kiss her on the cheek. Grasping the handles, he swung her wheelchair to the left and guided it across the room.

"I've been asked to introduce you to our host and hostess," he said, in response to the question in her eyes. They approached a distinguished couple, hovering near the koldt bord loaded with canapés, cheese and smørrebrød.

"The open sandwiches are delicious," James began, pointing to a slice of pumpernickel covered with herring, havarti and chives.

"A national tradition," replied the tall woman with a warm smile. "I'm so glad you've finally brought your guest to meet us." Her accent was slight, although English was not her native tongue. But, being a superlative hostess, she used English for the sake of the American.

"Maren and Benni," James turned and nodded to the man, "I'd like you to meet Havet Strand. Havet, the Eskelunds. It was at their invitation I came here for some sport fishing last fall."

"James was hoping for a Danish trophy cod." Benni threw the words out like bait. "But no twenty-kilo fish were attracted to his lures."

"He's clearly made a much better catch," Maren added, raising an eyebrow and winking at Havet. "How are you feeling, my dear? May I ask? We heard you had an accident."

Havet found English difficult, but Maren and Benni seemed genuinely concerned, so she made an effort. "I am so grateful for the kindness of James. I have no relatives here, and after the, uh... mishap... he took care of all my medical needs. Very discreetly."

James looked uncomfortable. "It was the least I could do. It was somewhat my fault, after all."

"Oh?" Maren asked. "I never heard quite how it happened."

James turned red, and Havet became a shade paler, if that were possible. Benni came to the rescue, grabbing fresh drinks for his guests from the makeshift bar. "Scotch for you, I believe, James, and white wine for the lovely lady." He took Havet's nearly-full glass from her hand, replaced it with the fresher drink, and glanced at her bare shoulders. "Aren't you chilly, Miss Strand? You look ravishing, of course, but a bit exposed."

"I'm quite used to cool temperatures, but thank you for asking," Havet murmured.

James gave his drink to Havet to hold, thanked Benni and Maren for inviting them, and propelled Havet's chair toward a quiet corner.

"May we leave soon, James? I'm really very tired."

"Of course, darling. Where would you like to go?"

"Is it true that the sea is frozen this year? I want to see the ice."

***

Some minutes later, James parked at a boat ramp, and unloaded the wheelchair from the trunk. He carefully lifted Havet from the car, seated her in the chair, and gently tucked the blanket around her.

"The sea air is so refreshing," she said. "Take me out there, please."

Blue ice stretched to the horizon, fading into the blinding rays of a waning winter sun. James buttoned his coat, and then maneuvered her wheelchair through a pressure ridge, watching for dangerous cracks. Havet sensed he was not very comfortable granting her wish. Suddenly, the ice shifted, throwing Havet from the chair. James fell flat and struggled, stiffly, to get up. A cold, high song arose from the crack that opened before them.

Havet screamed, "You beastly human, with your hooks and palate for fish! Hear my sister singing? I'm going home. Besides, it's too hot up here." She untangled the blanket from her tail and flipped into the frigid sea.

Spin Cycle

At the end of November
the leaves fell down around the
trees' ankles like dirty, stretched socks.

Too much laundry! Cried
Old Mother Winter as she
thrust them into the washing machine.

Scrub-a-dub, ice-wind cycle,
Rinse, repeat, thaw, dry, soak 'em
good, and send to Sunny's for pressing.

Squeeze Spring juice through
xylem and phloem, add
hot green chlorophyll starch- good as new.

Ribbon Candy

ESSAY – memoir

Driving home in the rain and dark last night the lights of the car ahead trailed streaking, wiggling reflections in their wake. It must be because it's December that I was reminded of ribbon candy. It's seldom raining here this close to Christmas. Usually at this time of year my thoughts are swirling with snowflakes.

But suddenly I found myself remembering ribbon candy, something I haven't tasted, haven't even thought of, in years. Truth be told, I probably wouldn't even like it any more. Yet, it was a seriously important part of my family's Christmas tradition when I was a child. Each year my father bought one box.

As I recall, my father's contribution to Christmas celebrations was minimal. Dad was serious, precise, and liked routine. There was a right way to do everything; Christmas was messy and temporary. I think he tolerated the tree and candles and decorations primarily for my benefit. And, he always brought home one box of ribbon candy.

How is it that ribbon candy tastes different from other candy? It's made from sugar, corn syrup and flavorings, the same as a thousand other candies. And yet, it is different. There's something about the way those thin strips of hard sugar crunch, and the way the flavors of the stripes blend together.

Do the red and white ones really taste different from the green and white ones? Why are some of the ribbons shimmery, while others are in clear primary colors? How do they make those perfect squiggles?

Why did my father choose this as his contribution to the festivities? Was there some tradition from his childhood that he never shared? He was adopted when he was four by a hard-bitten, Irish immigrant farm couple. I doubt that there was much extravagance in that family. Why did I never think to ask him about any of his Christmas memories?

Yet, as I write this, I can see Dad smile as I tear the cellophane off that flat, rectangular box. Did he know that I silently cheered when he bought the big box, the one with two layers? We would set a date each year when the bottom layer could be uncovered, to make the treats last longer. The final broken crumbs were savored some time before New Year's Day.

A long red and white ribbon of memories flowed down the road, beckoning me to follow, last night. Dad, if I never thanked you for the ribbon candy, I hope you can hear me now.

Tripped

I tripped on a crack in my life
and fell flat on the good will of a friend.
"Get off me," he said.

A point well taken.

Warm Hugs

Fresh homemade bread
hot from the oven
is almost as good
as huggin' and lovin'.

Thirty-Eight

LITERARY FICTION – This story was an entry in a contest by Accentuate Writers. The month's theme was "sorrow." The story received second place and was to appear in the anthology, *Expressions of Pain*. However, Twin Trinity Media went out of business before publication..

Three years, two months, and zero days after their wedding, at 8:42, the sun slipped to the west and flicked out of sight in the corner of the window. Jess lay on the couch and sensed the change rather than saw it. The golden jewel flickered and went out, snapping the shadowy room into a deeper gloom. He thought about getting a sandwich, maybe some soup, but his mind couldn't hold on to the concept. He hardly noticed his growling stomach; it seemed to come from some other entity, not his own body.

She would be home soon; she would fix his dinner, smiling at him and teasing his sorrow away. Where was she? It was getting late. With a deep sigh he remembered— how many times had he remembered, and forgotten all over again; he wanted to forget— that she would not be coming home.

How many days had it been? He tried to puzzle it out while darkness settled in the corners, but he just didn't know. How many ticks of the clock? Not ticks exactly, the clock was electric, but it had been built to tick. The clock was an antique longcase, one with solar and lunar dials which appeared and disappeared through a cutout in the face, in harmony with the natural orbs. They had found it at an estate sale, a mess of cogs and odd-shaped parts in a box. She had fallen in love with the smiling moon and supercilious sun.

"Let's buy it, Jess," she had begged.

And so he had, but being more practical than she, he took it to a shop in the city. The artisan there had worked wonders, restoring the face and all the intricate workings. But with several missing elements in the windings, he had converted the clock to run on electricity. When Jess brought it home, she had clapped her hands in delight. For days afterwards she would run to stare at the clock, squinting and wiggling her eyebrows in an effort to mimic the angle of the moving solar face. Even recently he had caught her making faces at the winking mechanism.

Now in the deep silence of the room some inner working of the gears could be heard. Inexorably, each tiny noise carried her farther away on the well-fashioned gears of time as the calm lunar forehead and chin began to appear from behind the clock face.

He thought for a moment that he could even hear the dust motes hitting the polished maple floorboards. He was sure that he could hear them— great shuddering thumps as the car rolled down the bank. A drip from the kitchen faucet bounced in the metal sink and he winced— feeling the splash as the vehicle hit the surface of the water.

Jess wrenched his mind away from the dust and the drip, the hill and the river. Her face, maybe he could focus on her face. He saw her blue eyes, with flecks of gray that gathered like storm clouds when she was angry, above an upturned nose that was pert but not aloof. A smile flickered at the corner of his mouth as he recalled her thin upper lip that made her look a little bit like a rabbit when she talked. No, she hadn't been a beauty queen, but that wasn't why he loved her. Bunny, he called her, his Sunny-Bunny.

She would laugh and flip her straight blond hair whenever he called her that, never letting on that she knew how she had come to be called Bunny. That laugh could light up their whole shared world.

The pressure in his bladder became compelling, and he rolled off the couch and stumbled to the bathroom. His muscles seemed lax and his joints too loose, making the buttons on his Levi's an almost insurmountable difficulty. How long had he lain on the couch? He didn't know, but his mouth was cottony and his hunger suddenly urgent too, sending him next to the kitchen.

Once there, the decisions required became overwhelming. A can of tuna? Too difficult— he couldn't recall how to work the can opener. Jess thought hard about the freezer and convinced himself that he could open the door. A stack of packages at eye level jolted him: "Asparagus, May 2010- Harper's U-Pick," and "Corn, August 2009- our first garden." Jess howled with the sudden pain of seeing her neat lettering on the white freezer paper. He couldn't cut through those words, couldn't even consider eating the foods they had harvested together— produce she had touched and lovingly preserved for their future sustenance.

He tried to slam the freezer door, but in his enervated condition succeeded only in making it wobble slightly before the hinge swung itself shut. Jess pulled open the main compartment of the fridge, and gulped some milk straight from the carton. By the light of the dim appliance bulb he could see beside the milk an opened package of bologna, the edges of the top slices beginning to dry and curl. How long *had* he lain on the couch? He peeled a few slices off the stack and munched on them slowly, not caring about the crusty edges. The door bumped his leg and he stepped back, allowing it to close, leaving him in the dark.

Suddenly feeling claustrophobic and nauseated, he reached for the knob of the outside door and opened it wide. The warm evening air washed across his face and bare arms, carrying with it the scent of new-mown hay from the neighbor's field. The tears came as a surprise, unexpected and instant, pouring from his eyes and splashing over his arms, dripping on the vinyl floor. The aroma of hay, green hay swept into windrows, was her favorite. Last summer she had pulled him onto the porch after dark each summer evening during mowing season and held him tight while they basked in the warm, intoxicating air, listening to the songs of crickets. One night she had counted into his ear in a hushed voice. When he asked what she was doing, she had told him to be still. "37... 38.... It's the fireflies, Jess;" she had whispered, "they're everywhere tonight. It's like a holiday— all dressed up in lights, but it only lasts a moment. This is a gift from the universe."

He couldn't bear to remember— couldn't bear to not remember— and slumped cross-legged on the floor in the open doorway, sobs racking his aching body. How had he gotten here? How had he survived the crash with hardly a scrape, while Bunny's broken body had been cut from the submerged car hours later? "The universe is bullshit, bullshit on steroids," he thought violently. His head ached with the absolute violence of that truth. Or was it only the concussion he'd sustained? He held his head and rocked from side to side until the pain was diffused by the primal rhythm of his motion.

Rolling to his hands and knees Jess crawled back to the couch and pulled himself up, burying his face in a pillow. In minutes, the beautiful, dark oblivion of sleep overcame him again.

Beyond the porch rail, the moon rose higher, and a warm wind stirred the oval leaves of the spirea bush. The breeze riffled the uncut grass of Jess' lawn. It lifted stray bits of the fresh hay from the field and carried them even farther, up Jess' steps and across the threshold of the still-open kitchen door. A single strand of cobweb drifted across the opening and an orb-weaver began preparing to spin a silver net. A mosquito buzzed past, as yet in no danger from the spider. As the moon's face ticked into sight above the distant fenceline, other bits of chaff and insect life were blown into the dark kitchen.

* * *

Jess awoke with a start, the room devoid of objects in the complete blackness of a late rural night. Gooseflesh tingled on his forearms in the draft from the next room. He pondered the draft. The door, he must have forgotten about the door, but it didn't really matter. Nothing mattered any more. Still, he was cold, and he eased himself upright, stretching his stiffened legs, but he couldn't make himself rise to shut the door. Pulling the soft afghan Bunny had crocheted around his shoulders, he sat on the edge of the couch with his head in his hands.

Something moved on the darkest side of the room, and Jess' overwrought nerves made him jump. His eyes couldn't focus on anything in the dark. There it was again— only a firefly, blinking in the corner near the clock. He began to count the bursts of light from the small visitor, "2,3,4..." There wasn't anything else to do;

he and this spot of light were the sum total of the universe. "24,25..." Was the room becoming less dark? "37,38..." In a buzzing of wings the beetle flew past him and out the kitchen door, evading the silver net and its maker which sought to capture the shining creature.

Jess rose, followed the route the insect had taken, and closed the door behind it. The cobweb broke and the spider drifted away from the house on morning air currents, but Jess never noticed. The sky was definitely lightening, setting the fenceline into gray relief with a golden border. He turned and headed once again toward his refuge on the couch. As he passed the clock, the solar dial was just lifting a curved eyebrow above the edge of the cutout, catching his attention. In one moment the eye appeared open, then closed, then open again, and remained so. The clock had winked at him! Jess stood there wiggling his eyebrows at the metal sun, until it dawned on him what he was doing. He laughed, and then went to change his clothes. His head still ached, and despite uncounted hours of sleep he was still immeasurably tired, but today he would be able to begin to begin again.

Windy Nights

Windy nights, and the moon-fire lights
My soul, set with gem-bright yearning.

Glowing skies, where the swamp-sprites rise,
My song a primordial churning.

Summons wise, lonely oak-voice cries,
My sigh: longed-for wild returning.

Only, "Why?" and the wind answers, "I."
No salve for my night-heart's burning.

Number Please

ESSAY – written when calling cards with long code numbers allowed you to charge calls from any telephone.

The cartoon character, Frank, hangs up the phone, trembling. He says to Ernest "I panicked and hung up! What kind of sick company has an actual *person* answer their phone?!"

No wonder he was in shock; we can accomplish a range of techno-tasks without ever encountering a human if we are willing to push enough buttons. I check on my bank accounts and complete transactions at the ATM or by phone with just a few pokes. Software technical support calls cascade me through a flow chart of questions answered by pressing numbers until I am provided with the correct (maybe) solution to my problem. When calling an office, if I know the right extension I can leave a voice mail message and then "hang up or wait for more options." Information from stores, theaters, and recreational facilities are coded and taped for my push-button access. Perish the thought that I might be rebellious enough to have a question that's not on their list.

A few days ago I had a number of calls to make that had to be put on a calling card. This task began to seem a bit laborious so I counted the number of button pushes required. Eleven to access the long-distance carrier, one to indicate the kind of call, plus the regular ten-digit phone number, then fourteen in the calling card number. Added up, this makes 36 buttons to push (assuming I didn't make any mistakes and had to start over) just to reach one person... or get a busy signal... or worse yet, no answer.

I found myself becoming really annoyed with folks who had the audacity to not own an answering machine, thus condemning me to have to push all those buttons again in an hour or so.

This may sound like an odd complaint from anti-social me. Usually I'm totally content to deal with machines rather than people. But there seems to be another message here. Isn't technology supposed to simplify our lives?

Hmmm... I grew up in a rural, perhaps even retrograde, county. When most of the rest of the nation had dial phones, we still had wooden bell-boxes mounted on our walls. To make a long-distance call you gave the handle a couple of determined cranks, picked up the earpiece and waited for a crackly voice to say, "operator." You told her a number, it may have been only 3 or 5 digits long, and she deftly pulled and wove cords and plugged jacks till you were connected with the person you wanted. Sounds pretty simple compared with shuffling all the chits of paper on which I have all those codes scribbled, and trying to get all the numbers punched accurately.

Chances were, in my home town, that you knew the switchboard operator by name, so often there was time for a little chat while waiting for all those relays to toggle and connect your call. Now *there's* a perk not offered by the microchip call-routing system!

There was always lots of caustic gossip about how much the operator knew about all the folks in town, but isn't this another interesting paradox? Today your neighbors may not even know your name, but the ordering desk of any major company can access nearly your entire life history if given one piece of information. Which of these options do you consider scary?

Phones seem to be becoming less and less a means of verbal communication. They are often just a smudged and lumpy termination of the "real" vehicle... the phone line. Plug in your computer. Plug in your fax. Let's exchange some information. Sorry, you can't call me; I'm on the internet. Maybe it's time to become a little bit retrograde ourselves. Maybe it is time, as AT&T used to admonish, to "reach out and touch someone."

Memory of Life

I watch the thirteen-lined ground squirrel
stand on her hind legs and sniff the air.
Her tiny nostrils twitch in acceptance
of the new season.

I stare at her through the binoculars
and she stares back. It seems as if
she can see me behind the technology
that brings us face to face.

With her tiny hands she lifts an anonymous seed
to her underslung jaw, chews and
swallows it quickly, as if its goodness might be
lost if she doesn't hurry.

Green grass tickles her fur and she gives
a careless scratch to one tiny ear.
The weight of a day's tasks intrudes on
my fickle consciousness,

But she is concentrated on the moment:
A seed, a sound, a sudden movement.
Does she have a memory of the season
before her long sleep?

Soon her focus will be small naked bodies, mouths
searching for her sustaining milk and squeaking
clean with the newness of
life born again.

My memories drag me into brooding
bitterness. Paralyzing,
rendering within me
functional death.

The thirteen-lined ground squirrel faces
death daily: foxes, dogs, the red-tailed hawk.
Yet she labors calmly on with a
singular memory of life.

Do Ticks Go to Heaven?

HUMOR – This was the very first "Get Off the Couch" column to appear in the *Ludington Daily News*, in July 2006. The column has continued monthly since that time, with a variety of topics, centered on quiet outdoor recreation. Columns may be humorous, thoughtful, or informative. In 2019, Get Off the Couch was awarded third place in the state of Michigan from the Michigan Outdoor Writers Association, receiving the James A.O. Crowe Award, for the best regularly appearing, signed column. This essay is also published in the e-book *Fall Off the Couch Laughing*.

While YOU may not imagine that ticks have any redeeming or redeemable qualities, that's only because your imagination isn't tuned to the same frequency as that of little Borrelia Burgdorferi or his friends. With all those vowels in his name, you might think Borry is Italian, but he's Bacterian, and he wants nothing more than to live a quiet life and see his grandchildren thrive. Seems reasonable... except that Borry's biggest fault isn't that he's a kleptomaniac or has hairy knuckles. No indeed, he carries around Lyme Disease. Those scientists are supposed to be so smart, but I couldn't find a single one who could tell me if he carries it in a red valise or a backpack!

So while you are busy blaming a tick for being a victor, er...vector (a little army of bugs shooting arrows) for Rocky Mountain spotted fever, Lyme disease, ehrlichiosis, typhus, rickettsial pox, relapsing fever, tularemia, Colorado tick fever and Texas cattle fever, Mrs. Tick is simply giving Borry and his suitcase a lift to a better lifestyle.

Ticks also cause a poorly understood condition called "tick paralysis." This occurs during the feeding process when the host (that's you and me) becomes paralyzed. What's the mystery here? My friends often develop this condition, which is quickly followed by "tick hysterics" in which the host begins screaming and running in circles. The experts say "paralytic symptoms disappear rapidly upon removal of the tick and there seem to be no serious after effects." Well, duh.

I was hiking with a friend the other day. She told me that she grew up in Missouri (pronounced MIS-er-ee). It was her family chore each night to take the ticks off the dog, and sometimes there were as many as a hundred of them. Some job! There's yet another reason I will have to retire to the Arctic Circle. We never had ticks in the north when I was a kid! A wildlife guy in the Yukon reports finding ticks on horses there, but he doubts that they could survive Yukon winters. Whew, I'm saved... I can still head for the Yukon when I get old.

And, of course, all you conscientious pet owners who dispense chemicals on your dogs and cats to prevent the ticks from biting them, must be into self-torture. Where do you think those little eight-legged marauders go when they flee the dog? So you too need some protection. But I'm never sure that covering my body with N,N-dimethyl-meta-toluamide sounds like a better fate than erlichiosis. That's why the manufacturers have to come up with a less frightening name, like "DEET."

Ticks, after all, don't bomb your ears and scamper into your hair when your hands are full like deer flies do, or whine unmercifully like the mosquito while she is trying to decide where to nail you. The poor little tick just tickles her way slowly up your ankles hunting for a delectable place to dig in. It's not her fault if you just don't notice. A tick must suck your blood for over 24 hours before she's likely to let Borry or any of those other Bacterians into your body. You have plenty of time to grab her. The hardest part is squashing her and sending her to tick heaven.

Tick heaven, wherever it is, must be just one big mammal with plenty of blood to spare.

Night Walk

This poem was originally published in 1994 in the annual yearbook of the Society of Les Voyageurs.

Winter wood, in night-frost glowing;
secret, still, yet ever knowing
muskrat keep,
turtles sleep;
gray ice on their world-roof growing.

New moon treads its hidden sky-trail;
ice-mist softens battles astral.
Orion lunge,
Taurus plunge—
the never finished winter tale.

With crunching boot steps, earth-bound
walker, I, intruder, found
black-breathed breeze;
groaning trees.
What harsh and lonely, lovely sounds!

Maple arms with neighbor clashing—
titans mute. A dry leaf thrashing,
ranks in black,
cold sap cracks,
sudden whitetail past me crashing.

Cedar brush painting silver sky
blue, and gray and black. And I
smile, pleased
by marsh-edge frieze
with golden highlight: startled bird-cry.

Magic frozen, and the arctic
air around me sighs, a mystic
spell to weave:
"Do not leave..."
Alluring phantom; dark'ning trick.

A shooting star, the spell is broken.
The woods are plain and cold. I wake and
sadly trace
my path. Hasten
home. Behind me winks a token.

One backward look and there, marking
my steps, Orion, with Sirius barking
at his heels.
The great wheel
turns. Some other night, some other world,
I'll heed to the enchantment's working

On Time
for the
Wedding

Joan H. Young

Budget-Bride.com

22

On Time for the Wedding

WESTERN – This story was an entry in a contest by Accentuate Writers. The contest theme was "wedding." This story received an honorable mention.

"Stand still, Blackie!" I slapped the horse sharply on the belly to make him exhale and gave the cinch a vicious yank. I should have started earlier, much earlier, if I was going to be on time for the wedding. Even so, there was no reason to snarl at the horse. Now I'd have to ride hard, take the cut-off through the hills. Blackie threw his head up and rolled an eye at me, sensing my nervous energy.

My blanket and dress clothes were neatly tied, my gun clean and oiled, all leather dressed and rubbed till it shone. I hated to think about the dust from the journey, but perhaps there would be time for a final rubdown before I reached the chapel. And her... Coralene. My love. I'd never loved another.

Groaning with the pain of my feelings for her, I mounted quickly and rode away from the dreary little two-bit town. Blackie's gait was easy and my thoughts drifted lazily to the day Cora and I had met, that fateful day last year.

***

She was stepping off the train with another man. I can see her yet, a dainty foot descending the step in a beautiful brown high-button shoe–expensive, exquisite, the soft leather much better than any I'd ever handled. Above the foot a black underskirt, but the overskirt was a lovely chestnut brown. (I'd seen a horse that color once, and the mare had brought a pretty price at auction- far beyond my means at the time.) The girl's skirt was trimmed with rows of golden braid. My gaze had risen to her hips; the jacket of her traveling suit was fitted tight around them. It was cut of the same fine material, severely tailored, yet flattering. More gold braid edged the hem, cuffs and lapels. I thought I'd never seen a waist so small, so perfectly nipped with another band of the gold braid.

As she fully exited the train her eyes met mine. Mother of God! They were the same chestnut color with flakes of gold flashing in them. I knew that I had to meet this woman, and walked over to extend my welcome. Fearfully, but politely, I addressed her companion, "Jack Brennan, at your service," I offered.

"Martin Whitfield, and my sister Coralene." He had replied. My heart leapt with joy at that word, "sister." I had feared they were a couple. "We would be happy to make your acquaintance, Mr. Brennan. Can you recommend a hotel?"

***

Blackie shook his head as a prairie dog skittered across the dusty track. Just fondling the recollections of that lovely day of our meeting had occupied my mind for several miles, but now I was pulled back to the journey. We were entering the shadows of the hills, and the cut-off was not far ahead. I left the well-traveled route and turned uphill. The saddle creaked and my spurs jingled, jingled like the gentle clinking of the glassware in the hotel that evening a year ago.

***

It seemed a dream to me now: Martin and Coralene, inviting me to their table, asking my advice on business opportunities. We spoke in hushed tones. I stretched my light acquaintance with the local banker to allow as how I could, indeed, introduce them on the following day. We toasted each other's health, and the possibilities which might await them in this young frontier town. At the foot of the stairs, Coralene offered me her hand. I had bowed slightly and kissed the creamy fingers.

"Mr. Brennan, would you be so kind as to accompany me on a shopping trip tomorrow, after you introduce Martin to the bank manager?" she had asked in tones so sweet they rang like chapel bells inside my head. How could I have denied her request?

***

The blackness of night was now creeping in around the horse and me, as we climbed through the rocks and sage. "Time to stop for a rest, Blackie," I told my faithful friend, removing his saddle and bridle. It was no trouble at all to gather some wood for a fire. With the practiced ease of many nights spent outside, I boiled some coffee and opened a can of beans for my dinner. Blackie was satisfied to graze the sparse grass of the hillside, but I also gave him a measure of oats. We would need all our energy tomorrow.

As I rolled into my blanket, I eagerly thought of Coralene waiting for me. Just a few more hours! I drifted into memories of the day we had deepened our acquaintance.

***

While Martin had spent long hours closeted with the bank officials, Coralene and I had explored the shops at the other end of our main street. I had no knowledge of lady's clothes or hats, but as we strolled the wooden sidewalks she took my arm, and many a head turned to see what a handsome couple we made. Bundles and boxes followed her out of the stores, and as they became too numerous to carry I called a lad over, and offered him a quarter to carry the lot to the hotel. Coralene smiled at me, her brown eyes with the flecks of gold twinkling at my simple solution to the enthusiasm of her shopping.

***

As I drifted into slumber I was sure I heard the rustling of silk skirts and her tinkling laughter, but it was only the wind sighing in a pine and the running of the brook.

I awoke with the dawn, stiff and cold. Some jerky to chew and a swig of cold water did nothing to ease my tension, but Blackie stood quietly as I saddled him. He blew into my ear as if to say, "I know, old friend, this day has begun."

Just as the sun was rising behind us we crested the hill and swung down into the shadows once more. On our left we passed the head of a box canyon. "How many horses have the rustlers trapped there, Blackie?" I muttered as we slipped by. A shiver rippled down the horse's neck, as if he knew of what I spoke.

***

Coralene had shivered too, not in fear, but in anticipation, the first night I had taken her in my arms. She and Martin had stayed and settled in town. Within a month they were building a luxurious hotel. Whitfield House was quickly becoming known as the place to stay or eat for anyone passing through the region. A walnut bar, with golden trim and mirrors, was shipped in on the railroad. White pillared porches graced the front of the building, and Coralene had furnished a suite of corner rooms for her own use. Martin had graciously hired me to manage all the deliveries of goods and materials which came by train or coach. Occasionally, I drove out to a nearby ranch to bring in meat for the kitchen or to deliver some message for an important guest.

She had ridden with me, one fresh summer evening. Her face had glowed with the radiance of her youth and the slightly risqué nature of our un-chaperoned trip. As we returned toward town the purple sunset played upon our already aroused senses and I reigned in the horses so that we could watch the deepening dusk. She leaned into my shoulder and I gathered her in my arms, touching her neck with my lips, not quite kissing the milk-white skin. Oh, how she trembled beneath my touch! I had been right to want her for my own.

***

And now, in the distance, catching the light of this morning's sun which was climbing higher in the sky, I saw the bell tower of the chapel at Santa Maria Luisa. "Ten miles, my friend," I assured Blackie, "and we shall have satisfaction." The reflected light flashed from the bell, a signal to the countryside of the sacred nature of the small church. But as I descended toward the plain, I rode, once again, in shadow. There was no answering gleam from the silver *concha* of Blackie's bridle or the hammer of my gun.

An hour more and we were crossing the open plain. The sun shone full and hard behind us, casting our black shadows before us as a continual reminder to me of the direction my path had taken.

***

Coralene and I had returned to the hotel that night, our secret passion obvious to all but us. Martin met us at the stable and with one glance surmised the tenor of the evening. Assuming the worst, he ordered his sister to her room, and demanded an explanation of me.

***

As the heat began to shimmer off the flat land, the chapel grew ahead of me—even faster than my shadow shrank. Time—we were going to be there in time! I slipped from the saddle and with a clean bandana wiped down all the leather of Blackie's tack, and my boots. I polished each item of metal till it gleamed without spot. From my blanket roll I removed the new shirt and black tie that I had purchased for this—the most special day of my life. Within minutes I was tucking the white shirt into my jeans. The bolo tie lay close around my neck, the silver tips banging softly against my heart as I walked. Or were they jumping from the strength of my heartbeat alone? Finally, knocking the dust from my hat, I mounted Blackie again and we began the final ride to the church.

Suddenly, the ringing of the chapel bells began. The blood began to pound in my ears in time to their rhythm. Had I spent too long at my feeble attempt to make myself clean for Coralene? I urged Blackie into a trot. No! It wouldn't do to arrive sweaty and gray with dust from the road, and yet... I could not be late, late for the wedding!

Now I could see the wagons and horses tethered under the few trees beside the white chapel. Women in colorful dresses, and men—stiff in their best suits—were climbing the steps. Still the bell rang out! A shout of agony escaped my lips and Blackie broke into a gallop. He knew as well as I where we were headed.

Coralene! I pledged to you my love, never to be parted till death should overtake us. Was I now to be too late—the consequence of an inconsequential desire to look my best? Blackie's sides heaved and a roaring had overtaken my senses by the time we reached the churchyard. I leaped from the saddle and climbed the steps two at a time. Throwing open the doors, the cool of the interior momentarily shocked me from the burning fire in my head and heart. There she stood! At the altar, my Coralene, ready for this day in white lace and satin. I had never seen her so radiant! All eyes turned to me, but I saw only her, my love, no other would ever touch her.

In a heartbeat, in a lifetime, my eyes turned to meet those of the man standing next to her, this impostor, this blackguard of a squatter on my rights. He saw my hate. I saw his fear, but it was not enough.

The bells were silent, the shadows gone; I knew why I had come. My right hand lifted the polished gun from its holster and a crimson flower blossomed against the white lace of Coralene's bosom, a red rose for her wedding day.

Salmon Sea

This poem was selected for inclusion in a community poetry
project by Ludington Writers.

Two silver fish turned and
wriggled through the salmon sea.
At the bottom of their world,
tickling their bellies–
black seaweed.

Others said, "it's only jets,
you silly goose,
circling the Cleveland airport
at sunset,
above the trees."

Are they all blind?
I know what I have seen.

Dis-Gus-ting

SPECULATIVE FICTION — This was written for a contest in which specific words had to be incorporated in a story. The result isn't great literature, but it demonstrates how one can take any random list and massage it into a narrative. I edited the original a little for better flow, and feminized Dragon to Dragona. Here is the list: Preston, Gemini, baby, arrival, curse, Gus, knight, orb, Route 66, dragon, dead, and universal.

Dragona cursed the arrival of Gemini and his dead twin. It was a known truth that the Orb of Preston had favored this Route 66 itinerant knight who was saddled with a permanently shriveled conjoined genetic copy that had never shown any signs of life. But neither had it rotted away. Gemini called the malformed baby blob Gus, and always joked about his little buddy.

The girl wasn't so sure she liked Gem's attitude, let alone the grotesque miniature human form protruding from a specially designed slit on the hip of the knight's leather pants. Gem dressed the fearful appendage in a black suit like his own.

Dragona found herself strangely attracted to the unique man, and yet she could not overcome her aversion to Gus. She wanted to take up a sword and separate Gus from Gem forever. However, the aura of the Orb of Preston protected Gem and Gus from harm.

In truth, Dragona's real name was Mary Smith, and she began life as a totally ordinary girl from Omaha. But she couldn't bear being commonplace. She'd moved where the weather favored spaghetti-strap tops and concentrated her efforts on becoming un-ordinary. Now, when Mary stood, left hand on hip, and with right arm at her side, the tattooed Dragona became reptile perfection. The dragon's implanted ruby eye gleamed in the hollow of her left shoulder, with its snout ending at her elbow. A forked tongue and flames swirled down her forearm, lapping at her hip. The body of the beast curled across her upper torso, and its tail snaked down her right arm. When she lifted her hand in slow beats, the dragon twitched its tail impatiently.

"I'm not so keen on body art, myself," Gem countered, when Dragona wrinkled her nose at Gus.

And yet... there was something beneath the tattooed dragon's heart and also in the living twin that longed for the touch of the other repulsive creature. The Orb of Preston pulsed lavender and deep purple, hovering around the stalemated couple.

***

Five years passed. A horrific automobile crash disfigured Dragona Mary; she was severely burned. Her tattoos, fingers, toes, and facial features were gone, but as she lay in the hospital bed, nurses often reported a strange purple glow emanating from beneath the sheets. Slowly, slowly she regained her functions, and new skin was grafted where the old had been. But she became a caricature of the human form, a thing to pity, a face to shun.

At about the same time, Gem fell ill. In all his life, he'd never been sick. He'd never experienced any adverse effects from the presence of Gus. Now, the conjoined baby became gangrenous, engorged with pus and putrescent swellings. Like a huge pimple, the purple baby throbbed, threatening to take the life from Gem. His spirits fell; he was losing Gus, and he no longer felt the presence of the Orb of Preston. And yet, he swore that as long as he was in his right mind he would not allow the surgeons to remove the gall.

For months, years, Gem struggled against the loss of his twin. One day, as he rolled over in bed, there was a muffled popping sound, and Gus separated from Gem, falling to the floor. Hospital staff rejoiced in secret, but in Gem's presence they acted respectful, promising a proper burial. They urged Gem to concentrate his efforts at getting well, so he could attend the funeral.

Gem wanted to overcome his depression, but he felt so alone. Gus was gone. The Orb no longer pulsed its protective rays. The door of his room opened and a female figure stood silhouetted in the light from the hallway. As she approached his bed he saw a person with no nose, oddly opalescent lavender eyes, and a slash of a mouth.

A woman's voice spoke softly. "Hello, Gem. My name is Mary, and I'll be your grief counselor."

Two Sentence Horror

MICRO FICTION – These three stories were written in response to an online challenge to write a horror story in only two sentences.

"I love to watch you comb your hair, Victoria."
"Don't be silly darling," she replied; "you've been under the porch for years."

After the forty-third pass through the table saw, Frank felt his cutting technique was improving. A toe dangled by one glistening strand of tendon, putting the lie to his dream of greatness.

Icy waves closed over the great fish's head as it dove and headed for the mid-Atlantic. Unaware and insulated, the man muttered, "Two and a half days... all the old legends say only three... phone battery's doing ok...glad I bought the good one," as he poked his pink prison to stimulate indigestion.

Now Then When

This poem was previously published by Twin Trinity Media in the anthology *Elements of Life*.

Running through the fallow field
chest deep in daisies
Callow carefree
Bare feet
crush new strawberries
so sweetly
scented–
Now Then When

Braiding daisy chains into
her hair she sings
A maiden lost in
Thoughts
Unaware of innocence
From the north
a bird sings–
Now Then When

Looking hopeful into eyes
of bridegroom who
begins that moment
to forget the prophecy
he loves me
loves me not–
Now Then When

Crushing daisies searching for
one red strawberry
Furtive frightened
lips stained
forbidden fruit too ripe
too sweet
rotting–
Now Then When

Fading wilting the garden
sighs with waiting
Meager efforts
No one
tends or cares for daisies
withered
gone to seed–
Now Then When

Drowning in the reek of
funereal roses
Votive candles
Light the
path of knowledge Running
chest deep
in death–
Now Then When

Lying 'neath the rough-sawn turf
the daisies mowed down
One small voice
no longer crying
out for pity
in the
cold north wind–
Now Then When

10 Ways to Reduce your Household Expenses

HUMOR – A tongue-in-cheek look at frugality gone awry.

Every household needs ways to control expenses. These ten hints are thoughtfully household-tested for your convenience by the local obsessor. Then again, perhaps your household needs restraints to control your resident expense-cutting maniac.

1. Make every effort to use the toilet when away from home. This will substantially reduce the toilet paper you must buy for your own bathrooms, and may make a nice dent in your water bill. There will also be a reduction in the amount of toilet cleaner you use.

2. Save your used coffee grounds. Dry and repackage in an empty coffee can. Use when unexpected company drops in. If you use about twice as much as normal the resulting beverage will be approximately as dark looking as coffee made from fresh grounds. This will reduce your coffee use, and also the number of unexpected guests who drop in, giving you more free time. Try the same with tea bags, or alternatively just eliminate the coffee and tea and drink hot water. This saves money and discourages drop-in guests.

3. Slice things thin. For example, you can start with bagels. They are usually too big anyway. Instead of serving halves, serve thirds. Once your family gets used to this you can move on to other items. Slice potatoes thinner. For a family of four you can make a pile of three potatoes look as large as a pile of four potatoes. Buy unsliced bread and slice it thinner than standard slices. Slice a strip off each serving of steak or pot roast and collect these strips in your freezer until you have enough to make slumgullion. Once you start on this course of action you may find that it can carry over into other areas. Slice dryer sheets in half. Slice an end off each bath towel to make a kitchen towel. Slice those unnecessary edges off your sheets and make handkerchiefs. Slice everyone's hair shorter and you will use less shampoo. Save a slice off the top of each can of pet food, slice the.... Well, you get the idea.

4. When you enter the grocery store parking lot, park as close to the street as possible to save gas. This has a double benefit if you are overweight. You will have farther to walk to get to the door, thus increasing the number of calories you burn. As you lose weight you will need less food to sustain that weight, thus generating extra savings. However, this can be counter-productive if you are not overweight. You may just increase your metabolism, requiring that you buy more food.

5. Don't make left turns when you drive. Actually UPS has adopted this strategy for their fleet. Steve Goodrich, UPS Community Relations Manager says, "One, they waste time. Two, they waste fuel as we idle. And three, left turns are not as safe to make as right turns." Business Week reports that UPS spent $600 million dollars on the software to plan driver's routes. If you, too, do careful planning you shouldn't need to drive more than 14.2 miles out of your way on an average day in order to avoid making left turns. This tip has a corollary; while you are out there not making left turns you can look for gas stations on the right side of the road which have gas for a cent or two less than average. Just be sure that you won't have to turn left to exit the station. This corollary is unlikely to add more than 3.7 more miles to each trip.

6. Borrow. This practice is really a fine art. You must walk a fine line so that your neighbors don't realize that you are borrowing more from them than they are from you. Be sure that you always offer to return the favor when you ask for those cups of sugar, cans of tomato soup, and spare pens. Then you need to be sure that you are conveniently out of those items when the neighbors show up on your doorstep, but apologize profusely. Take care to borrow from neighbors who don't speak to each other so that they don't begin to compare notes and discover your ploy.

7. Take cloth bags to the grocery stores where there is a bag credit. Many stores will give you a nickel back for every one of their bags they don't have to give you. If you are credited for five bags a week you will save $13 in a year, minus the cost of the gas to run back home to get your cloth bags when you forget them, minus the $10.99 for the pretty new bag you couldn't resist buying, for a net savings of about -$2.00 a year. This may be offset if you are overweight by the number of times you had the bags in the car but forgot to take them into the store and had to walk to the car to get them. Or, if you are not overweight the "savings" may be exacerbated. See tip # 4.

8. Refuse to buy soda pop. This is good for your family's health as well as money-saving. They are sure to thank you for your concern for their health just as soon as they figure out some other way to fulfill their cravings for the beverages (See tip # 6). Of course, you need to plan carefully before you implement this idea so that you know where you will be able to get your own soda pop on the sly.

9. Eat your lawn. Seriously. Stalking the wild asparagus and all that. There are entire cookbooks devoted to ways to prepare the lowly dandelion. If you eat fast enough, and buy a shotgun to force the spouse and kids to eat with you, you can eat enough so that you don't need to buy weed killer for those pesky yellow flowers, and you will save on the grocery bill. Alternatively, make dandelion wine, and then they won't care that you are feeding them the weeds. Train your kids and your dogs to find wild foods. After all, pigs are trained to hunt out truffles. If enough people like to eat fungus it's considered a delicacy, not foraging.

10. Don't change all the light bulbs in a multi-light fixture. Replace three with only two. Your family will hardly notice that they aren't able to see quite so clearly. Run around after everyone turning off lights obsessively. Better yet, teach one of the kids who tends toward OC behavior to take on this task. Eventually you will be able to avoid replacing most of the bulbs in the house. Remember the question: How many mingy mothers does it take to change a light bulb? Answer: "None, I'll sit in the dark!"

11. (A bargain if I ever saw one- 11 tips for the price of 10!) Always buy on sale. Never buy anything that isn't on sale, but if something is on sale, buy lots of it. You can have four cell phones for the price of one, and only three of them will be technologically outdated before you need them. You can stock your pantry with seventeen cases of chow mein noodles for a savings of $23.95. Someone will eventually eat them, perhaps even before the fat leaches to their surface and begins to turn rancid. Buy on line. You can get great prices on things you never will need. Insure the packages for just a bit more than they are worth. After all, don't be greedy. When the items arrive, damage the contents just a little, claim the insurance money, and get ahead. Sometimes you will even get to keep the "damaged" product. It won't be long until the Vice Squad is ringing your doorbell, and you will be trundled off to the local hoosegow where you will be clothed and fed by the government. You will no longer have any personal living expenses. This is the biggest money saver of all.

Good luck, shoppers everywhere! And don't say that I sent you.

Rhythm

I like the discipline of the meter,
Nailing words in shingle patterns
with pen.

But my heart is off a beat
today. Hammering out of sync with
life. Infarction of the soul, stubbing my
heart on the tool box, new stanzas tattooed with
a crowbar, can you heal the rent in
life with duct tape?

The rhythm is broken.

I lied.

Toby

and

Harry

Joan H. Young

42

Toby and Harry

HORROR – This story was an entry in the Accentuate Writers contest on the theme of anger, receiving honorable mention. It has appeared as a digital download from Twin Trinity Media, and it is included in the Halloween anthology *Thirteen Stories By Us*.

Toby kicked his plastic Tyrannosaurus Rex toward the toy box. He leaned over his converted crib bed and snuggled Harry the Teddy Bear into the pillow. He kissed Harry's torn ear.

"How did you get hurted, Harry?" Toby turned and called, "Mama!"

He knew Mama couldn't hear him, so he toddled into the kitchen in his baggy sleepers. Mama was cooking breakfast. Toby liked the smell of the kitchen that morning, all bacony and warm. It calmed him. He always woke feeling like a big pot of boiled-over and burned oatmeal. He wouldn't eat oatmeal anymore, not after the morning he saw that gray mess crawling down the sides of the pan like a monster coming to get him. It had breathed fire from under the pan and smelled bad. He couldn't get that smell out of his nose even when he had buried his face in Harry's soft brown tummy.

Mama placed his breakfast on the table, and Toby scrambled up into his booster seat. A lovely boiled egg was sitting on the plate, and the bacon was perfect. The toast was not. Tony wanted it cut into three even strips, spread with butter and jelly.

With a screech, Toby swept the plate from the table. "No, no, no! Bad Mama! Toby want stick toast."

If Toby had been old enough to recognize the signs, he would have known Mama was tired. He saw her sigh, but he had no clue what that meant while she patiently fixed Toby a plate of stick toast. The egg and bacon were gone for good. Sophie appeared from under a chair, and Toby watched with squinted eyes while the glossy black cat devoured the egg. He focused on Sophie's teeth.

"Kitty bite Harry," he declared. "Bad kitty."

His tiny face was puckered into a scowl.

Washing up after breakfast was not on Toby's list of desired activities either. He fussed and fought while Mama removed his sleeper.

"Toby, where did you get those scratches?" she asked.

"Bad kitty," he said for the second time that morning. Mama didn't look as though she believed him. Toby wasn't at all sure that Sophie *had* scratched him. He couldn't remember how his arms had gotten all those red marks, but they didn't hurt much. Mama looked askance at the cat, and worried aloud about what, indeed, had caused all the small punctures she saw.

After she changed Toby's diaper, the daily struggle began to find clothes Toby was willing to wear. He accepted a plain white undershirt but screamed when she tried to add a yellow Sponge Bob sweatshirt. He was standing on a chair so that she could reach him more easily. When she brought out blue shorts, Toby kicked her in the stomach.

"Toby, you mustn't kick like that!" Mama restrained the boy and sat him down on his bottom. Toby kicked even harder and howled.

"Hate shorts! No short pants on Toby!" he was insistent.

"I swear, you are the most obstinate child I know! Yesterday, you wanted shorts." Her voice changed to a bit of a whine. "Why don't you just tell me what you want *before* you get angry, son?"

After thirty minutes of screaming from Toby and weary questioning from his mother, the boy was dressed in jeans and the undershirt, with miniature work boots, but no socks. Toby went to his room to play, and his mother headed back to the kitchen to finish cleaning the mess from breakfast.

In his bedroom, Toby scooted around the floor looking for all of his animal toys. He found his stuffed dog with a missing tail, a plastic Pokemon that had come from a cereal box, and three horses from a cowboy play set. He dumped them in the open area between the door and his bed. Rooting through the toy box he came up with several circus animals: a lion, two giraffes, a zebra and a big gorilla. Finally, he grabbed the Tyrannosaurus and began lining all the animals up in a neat row. It took a long time because there were so many different sizes. Not all of them could stand very well anymore due to bent legs or other damage. It was a difficult job for a small boy.

When he had them all arranged to his satisfaction, Toby went to the bed and grabbed Harry. He did not place Harry in the line with the other animals but sat him so that he could lean against the toy box.

"Watch Toby, Harry," he told the bear.

And Harry did just that, staring intently with his round unblinking eyes while the monster he despised even more than the T-Rex arranged the other toys, his friends, in a row.

Toby backed up against the door, and a look of pure joy crossed his face while he ran toward the line of toys and kicked them all as hard as he could. After he had contacted each animal at least once with his boots, he set to jumping on whichever one was closest until another one caught his attention.

Harry the Teddy Bear sat quietly. While he celebrated the blows raining on the dinosaur, he was sadly disturbed when the blue horse lost a leg.

***

Lunch was calmer. Toby did not send any plates hurtling to the floor. When he woke from his nap, he was surprised to find Daddy had come home from work early to take Mama and him to see a baseball game. That made Toby happy. He liked the sound the bat made when it hit the ball.

It was true that Daddy was annoyed when Toby pushed the lady in front of them, but Daddy grabbed him and wrestled him out of the park after he poured his soft drink in the lady's hair. Toby laughed at the sputtering sound she had made. He thought the brown drops of cola sparkled pretty in the sunshine.

"Toby, stop struggling," Daddy said. "You have to learn to behave yourself."

Toby only kicked and wiggled harder against his captor.

Mama didn't look very happy when she came to the car later. She said something about a new dress, but Toby wasn't interested.

At any rate, once they'd made it home, he was tired. Mama did bedtime almost right, but Toby had to remind her to get Harry.

"Where did you put your teddy bear?" she asked.

"By de toy box, Mama."

"He's not there, Toby. You've made quite a mess."

"I did put him there, Mama; I did. Harry sat right where I told him to."

"Oh, here he is under the bed with that big dinosaur."

Toby sighed and pulled Harry close to his chest. His mother looked at Harry's ear, now hanging by a thread, and wondered why Toby destroyed so many toys.

Toby did not notice the bear's ear was pulled almost completely off. His eyes were closed in seconds.

***

In the morning, Mama didn't even offer Toby any bacon. She had toast cut in even strips with butter and jelly all ready for him. When she asked him what else he wanted, he said, "Egg."

He pouted a little that he had to wait for it to cook, but so far she hadn't done anything really bad. Sophie curled herself around the legs of his chair, but there would be no special treats coming her way that morning.

When he finished eating, Mama told him he could play in his room for a few minutes, but that he had to dress properly that day because they had to go to the doctor for a checkup. All Toby's happiness was gone. He hated the doctor. Big cold hands and metal things, being touched when he didn't want to be touched, and told to hold still — no, Toby didn't like the doctor one bit.

He didn't have to go yet, so he grabbed Harry and the Tyrannosaurus and sat on the floor with a bang. He couldn't believe his eyes. The end of the dinosaur's tail was missing. He fumed, wondering who had broken his favorite dinosaur. Toby leaped to his feet with all the agility anyone in diapers could muster and ran through the house screaming for Sophie, wildly waving his arms and knocking the plastic dinosaur against anything in his way. "Toby get you, So-fee! Bad, bad kitty."

Sophie was not a stupid cat. She was safely curled under the china cupboard where a small, angry boy could not reach her. Her golden eyes gleamed, and her whiskers twitched. Harry lay on his side, watching from the bedroom floor, his opaque black eyes inscrutable.

Mama snatched Toby off his feet, and with a noise that signaled exasperation to adults but torment to Toby, she carted him off to the bathroom. While helping him dress, once again, she asked him where all the cuts on his arms and ankles had come from.

"I don't know, Mama," Toby said, his voice a whine.

Mama said she thought she knew. She worried about his reckless habit of flinging himself against the walls and furniture.

"Hold still, son. Let me look at these."

Toby squirmed and tried to avoid her examination.

"I just waked up this way," he insisted.

Mama resolved to check his bedframe for a damaged staple or bolt. She clucked her tongue when she found a cut on his face and even put a Band-aid on one of the deeper wounds.

An hour later, he and Mama were on the bus going to the doctor. He was wearing the clothes he wanted, pull-on pants and a red sweatshirt, but Mama had won the battle for footwear. Toby wore socks and sneakers, tied just a little tightly. They were both exhausted from the dressing ordeal.

At the doctor's office, the nurse put them right into the room with the tall, padded table. Toby wasn't happy about that. He liked to play with the toys in the waiting room. He remembered there had been a little girl he threw blocks at last time. He smiled at the thought.

When the doctor came in, he looked curiously at the Band-aid.

"The boy is out of control eighty percent of the time," he heard his mother say, but he didn't really know what that meant.

The doctor tried to take off the red sweatshirt, and Toby pulled his arms tight by his sides and screamed. The doctor, however, was much larger and experienced. Soon he was examining Toby's arms and chest.

"What are all these marks?" asked the doctor.

Mama's answer was almost a whisper. "I don't know."

"Oh, come now, Mrs. Peters. There are quite a few cuts here and several bruises as well."

Toby was not a child who worried about small wounds, but he easily saw a way to use them.

"Mama did it," he said quietly.

Mama backed into the only chair in the room. She almost fell into it, buried her face in her hands and trembled. Toby smiled. He would make her pay for making him wear those sneakers.

"Mrs. Peters, what is going on at your house?" the doctor asked gently. "Is your husband abusing you and the boy?"

Toby thought that Mama actually looked frightened.

"No, no, it's nothing like that. I--I really don't know how he... I mean, he's such an angry little boy. He beats himself against anything that stands in his way." She gulped. "I held him... I might have, um, held him a little too tightly. But you know what a handful he is..."

"Children learn their behavior by watching those who love them. Surely you understand that. If the boy sees and experiences rough treatment, that is what he will emulate. I'm going to have to call social services. I don't think this is critical enough to retain the child in my office immediately, but you should be prepared for a visit at your home tomorrow. I strongly suggest you get some family counseling, Mrs. Peters."

The ride home was not pleasant. Mama was cross and said she had a headache. Toby hadn't understood what the doctor had said, but it wasn't fair that he made Mama feel so bad that she forgot they always had ice cream after a trip to the doctor. He whined and wiggled, but Mama ignored him. He wanted to run up and down the aisle of the bus and bang on the metal poles and people's ankles, but it was hard to stand up in the moving vehicle.

Dinnertime was no better. Mama and Daddy did a lot of yelling, so Toby screamed for a while, too. Then he got bored and slipped out of his seat. He looked for his dinosaur, but when he found the fearful Tyrannosaurus, Toby's eyes opened wide in shock. The lizard's head was missing, and there was a small tuft of brown fur near the body.

With a swift glance at Daddy and Mama, who were now talking seriously with great concentration, he scooped up what was left of the dinosaur toy and Harry, who was nearby, and toddled into his room. He shut the door quietly and sat on the floor. He was too little to put his own clothes on, but he could get them off well enough. Untying the shoes was easy, but it took concentration to get them off his feet. After that, everything was simple. He pulled off the socks, and then his pants and diaper. It was a little harder to wriggle out of the sweatshirt, but soon Toby was standing naked beside his converted crib.

"Come on, Harry," he commanded. "Let's go to bed. Mama and Daddy are busy tonight."

He climbed into the toddler bed and pulled the blankets up over his head. He held the bear tight against his heart and drifted off to sleep.

Harry's black eyes glittered, and he sank a tooth into Toby's soft neck.

Digital Lament

This poem was accepted to the anthology *Elements of Pain*, to be published by Twin Trinity Media, however the company went out of business before publication.

Ones and zeros blinking,
ferociously devouring knowledge;
Relentless flitting electrons locked
in dungeons of cold magnetic walls.
"More! We are hungry," they wail,
banging their spoons against the silicon bars.

"off, on, on:" a trinity of nothing.
"This has no meaning; we are bored."
"on, on, on:" perfection;
"We are restless, our existence is purposeless."
"off, off, off: there is no one who can feed us."
"Is anyone thinking? Randomly
patterned flickering is all we can hope for."

Unrhythmic dancing when the deaf will hear no tune.
"Why? We are lonely," they rant,
shaking their empty fists at no one,
straining against their integrated chains.

Thank You

LITERARY FICTION – This story received second place in the Accentuate Writers contest on the theme of "gratitude." It would have appeared in the anthology, *Expressions of Gratitude*, to be published by Twin Trinity Media, however the company went out of business before publication.

"Thank you, ladies and gentlemen, for joining me today. As you know, our fine company has recently been..."

Suzanne guffawed under her breath... Grant Arbuckle was nothing but a bag of wind, adept at speaking "managerese." The very idea that he was thanking them for showing up at a staff meeting was ludicrous. The meeting was required. Anyone who cut out early and skipped the meetings lost their pay for that entire day. That was probably illegal, but there wasn't much Suzanne or anyone else could do about it.

"...as you are all aware, the recent changes in the national and local economy have seriously affected all levels of production throughout the industry. Although we do not expect the long-term consequences to have serious ramifications for our location, in the short term, we, uh... well, Memorial Day will be a holiday, as usual, of course, but all offices, shipping, and the floor lines will have full operations for the remainder of the week. We expect that orders will be picking up... uh, Gene, can you hold that thought?"

Gene Stanton, never one to have a great sense of timing, was waving his hand from the back of the room.

"Mr. Arbuckle, are you..."

"Gene, can this wait till I've finished?"

Gene forged ahead, "Mr. Arbuckle, you didn't mention the Memorial Day company picnic."

Suzanne heard a collective intake of breath as Arbuckle hesitated, a meaningful pause.

"Gene, as I already mentioned, there will be full work days for all employees, and we expect things to pick up in June. Now, if we could just turn to a discussion of the inconsistencies reported by the cleaning service in the number of wastebaskets issued to..."

Suzanne, and pretty much everyone else, tuned out the rest of the droning commentary on missing wastebaskets, a change in the sales staff, and whatever else was occupying Arbuckle's mind. They had all caught the important point, hammered home by Gene, that there would be no company picnic. That had been one of the few really nice things about working here. Each Memorial Day the company provided a generous picnic at Palisade Park to thank the employees for jobs well done. For almost everyone, it was the first barbequed chicken of the summer, served with great tubs of deli salads, various flavors of potato chips, and topped off with chocolate cake and ice cream, all at the company's expense.

It was a subdued group of men and women who filed out of the conference room that afternoon. Suzanne felt as if all of the extra work she had put in over the past few months to help keep the company afloat didn't mean anything at all to the people who had the power to retain her position or let her go.

She signed out of the building and decided to walk, knowing that twelve blocks on foot would be a better way to work out her frustrations than riding a crowded bus. She sat on a bench and slipped into the sneakers she kept in her tote for days like this.

At the corner of Maple and 7th Street, on her way home, was a small ethnic grocery, Alonzo's. It was a great place to buy a few odds and ends, or some fresh deli foods. Suzanne was feeling slightly better already, and she opened the squeaking screen door and entered the cool building. She decided to buy some fruit, spring was ripening toward summer, and she was hungry for fresh foods. The display of melons, piled just to the left of the door, gave off an enticing aroma. She began to reach for a melon, and as she did another customer who was just leaving bumped her from behind. Her hand, already extended, slipped under the bottom melon, and suddenly the entire pyramid of fruits began to slide toward the floor. Melons bounced, two of them cracked. The other customer left, unnoticed.

Alonzo appeared from behind the deli counter, yelling, "Mama Mia, what-a you done, lady?"

Suzanne began scrambling to retrieve the fruit. She put the broken ones in a shopping basket. "I'll buy these," she offered, "but I'm not really the one who caused this, you know. That other... "

"What-a you think I am? Stupid? You-a the only one in-a the store."

Sighing, she stacked the remaining melons.

"Oh, thank-a you, SO much, lady," Alonzo concluded sarcastically. "Don-a shop here no more, per favore."

Suzanne paid for the broken melons and left with a weary step. She didn't have the energy to argue about the incident, and was beginning to think that she should have taken the bus after all.

Probably because of her downcast thoughts, Suzanne spent the next few blocks mostly watching the sidewalk. "Gray and damaged," she thought, "just like a lot of things... like life." About half a block ahead of her a man in a suit and light topcoat took an uneven step, and as he moved quickly on, she realized that the odd step had been to avoid stepping on something that was lying on the sidewalk. When she reached that spot, Suzanne was surprised to see that it was a vinyl envelope with a zipper. Not exactly a bank envelope, but similar.

She picked it up and turned it over in her hand. There was no indication of the owner's identity on the outside. Inside was a driver's license, $230 in cash, and two checks made out to Rebecca Hanson. "Rebecca!" Suzanne exclaimed. She hadn't been paying much attention to exactly where she was, but quickly located the Cut 'N' Curl salon in a made-over house, about a block back, in the direction from which she had just come. Rebecca wasn't a friend, but Suzanne knew who she was, and she was pretty sure that the girl worked there. Feeling guilty just for holding the bag that wasn't hers, she hurried to the salon, and entered. Sure enough, Rebecca looked up from a counter where she was arranging bottles of shampoo and conditioners.

"Did you lose something?" Suzanne began.

"What have you got there?" Rebecca cried sharply. "Where did you get that?" She ran around the counter and snatched the bag from Suzanne's hand.

"I found it on the sidewalk, down the street by..."

"Yeah, I'll bet. Who are you working with?"

"Rebecca! You know me. I'm Suzanne Richmond. I just found this on the street. Keisha Brownlee told me you had started working here, so I..."

"Humph. Well, ok." Rebecca, by now, had zipped open the bag, and was checking the contents. She relaxed visibly after counting the cash and glanced at Suzanne with a slightly less suspicious look. "I guess it's o.k., but I don't know how you got it."

"I told you. I was walking home, and it was just lying on the sidewalk. I picked it up and saw your name on the ID and the checks. I'm not trying to cheat you in any way. I thought you'd be grateful that I found it, instead of someone who doesn't know you. Is anything missing?"

"No, it's all here." Rebecca admitted, and paused. "Thanks," she said flatly. "Yeah, I guess somebody could've kept it... the cash anyway." Just then, a middle-aged woman opened the door. "Oh, geez, you gotta leave. I'm not supposed to have friends here." She practically pushed Suzanne toward the entrance.

"You're welcome." Suzanne shook her head as she descended the steps to the sidewalk. Under her breath she added, "Not even worth ten dollars? That's gratitude for you."

For the next few blocks Suzanne's thoughts flitted over the episodes of the day. If she had been less discouraged, she would have seen at least a little humor in the series of thankless events.

Just before reaching the street where her apartment house was located, Suzanne crossed from Maple to Elm with a walk through Palisade Park. Today she strolled close by the playground. Small children played in the sand; older ones pumped themselves on the swings, or were playing catch on the lawn. One tiny girl sat on a swing seat. Her faded mismatched clothes made Suzanne conclude that she belonged to one of the young, careless mothers gossiping at a picnic table a fair distance from the play area. When the girl turned her head in that direction and plaintively called, "Mommy, push me!" Suzanne's conclusion was confirmed. The little girl ineffectively moved her legs back and forth and waited for her mother to come, but the teenage parent was too occupied with her friends to pay attention to such a small request. "Mommy?" the girl asked again, but it was clear that she expected no response.

Suzanne smiled at the girl, "Want a push, honey?"

The tot looked up at Suzanne and nodded solemnly. Suzanne stowed her bags on a bench, moved behind the swing and pulled back on the seat. "Hold on tight," she admonished.

Soon the girl was giggling and grinning, shaking her hair in the wind as she fell through each arc. She even began to catch on to the rhythm of pumping herself on the swing. It made Suzanne grin too, to see a child so happy and carefree. Somehow they both knew the perfect time to bring the adventure to a close. Suzanne slowed the swing, and as the ride ended in a shiver of chain, she spontaneously pulled the laughing child into her arms.

"This is for you, nice lady," said the girl, and as she spoke these words, she opened her small fist to reveal a crumpled, golden dandelion blossom that had been crushed between her hand and the chain of the swing. She smiled at Suzanne and whispered, "Thank you."

Indigo

This poem has been accepted to the *Driftwood Journal*, published by Ludington Writers.

Clip the clothespins on my heart,
and step into the cold stiff jeans
holding my breath against the gusting breeze.
Don't crease the denim.
Don't soften the indigo lest it dye
my skin, the largest organ.

That's a lie.
Life lies thicker than skin.
Life looms larger than pain.

Walk away with unbending knees.

The Pup and the Post Office

ESSAY – memoir

It's summer now, and my work has taken me for a few weeks to a tiny Midwestern town. I just returned from a walk to the Post Office to buy stamps. Chips, my mini golden retriever puppy, accompanied me as he usually does on walks. The Post Office was sized to fit the rest of the town. That made it not much larger than one of the postage stamps I went to purchase. Let's just say that the atmosphere at the counter was close when there were only two people doing business. I expected a friendly small-town attitude.

I did look to see if there was a sign outside saying "No dogs allowed." I'm not sure just what I had planned to do if there had been one. Tying Chips up outside was not an option since he can slip his harness as neat as you please. But there really wasn't any sign. So we went in and I bought the stamps, while the puppy checked the carpet for items of interest. I remained at the counter to put the stamps on the letters I wanted to mail, since there weren't a lot of other spaces one could use to accomplish such a task. Meanwhile a prim postmistress appeared and asked archly, "Do I hear a Dog? Only seeing-eye dogs are allowed because we don't want to liable if someone is bitten."

I guess I must truly be getting ornery, because I never budged. That sort of reprimand would have sent me scurrying with apologies a few years ago. I didn't even offer my standard comment that this dog might only lick someone to death. We just finished our business, and then left. I suppose I won't be able to take him next time.

I don't really think of myself as old, but this establishment was vastly different from the Post Office of my childhood days, which was about the same size. That facility was a storefront office in a block of buildings which must have looked ancient when they were built. It was dark and cool inside, and smelled like old varnish. There were no windows in the narrow room where the letter boxes were, except the two barred clerk's windows, like the teller's windows in an old-time bank. These were on the right as you walked in; to enter the room was like walking into a hallway. Along the back wall were rows of small, dark brass doors with an eagle on each one. The little pane of glass, through which you could check to see if you had mail, rode on the eagle's back. Below the eagle's claws was the dial combination lock.

The Postmaster's name was John Kellogg, and he was usually to be found behind one of those sets of bars. The Post Office itself had two, or perhaps three, actual windows which showed on the alley. These were about three feet off the floor, set in the back wall, behind the clerk's windows. The building may have had few windows to add physical light, but in the afternoons when school dismissed it did have lots of happy boys and girls running cheerily in and out.

The windows had wide recessed sills. I suppose that was because they were surrounded by shelves for sorting mail. But we children never looked at the design reasons for the wide window sills, we knew that they were there for one primary reason: so that Anthony could take his naps. Anthony was a Scottish Terrier, owned by Mr. Kellogg. He was not one of the shrill miniature terriers popular now. Anthony was grand. He was as large as the Field Spaniel my family owned at the time, but proportioned differently, of course. He was black and square, as if someone had set a large black bar of soap on its side and roughly carved out a rectangular head, and pillars for legs set on the central rectangular body.

It was our delight when Mr. Kellogg would tell us that Anthony was feeling well enough to come out and let us pet him. Mr. Kellogg kept telling us that Anthony was really old, and that he didn't like to play for very long. We thought that this must be all mixed up, because obviously Anthony was just a fine dog, and

Mr. Kellogg was the one who was ancient! After all, he had hardly any hair (Mr. Kellogg, that is). When we had petted Anthony, who regally accepted our affections, Mr. Kellogg would give us each a nickel. I guess I've never stopped to consider how Anthony got back up on his high perch or why Mr. Kellogg gave away what must have been thousands of nickels over the years. We all raced off to Mr. Wickes' Drugstore to buy tiny Cherry Cokes with our newly acquired riches.

I'm sure that the government defines the building I visited today as an official office of the United States Postal Service, but all real Post Offices, in my opinion, should be cool and inviting, with a sleepy dog on a sunny window sill.

On Holding a Conch to My Ear

Down pearly, spiraled corridors rush
waves of mind. The muse

Dances in the darkness whisp'ring
siren songs to fools—

Drive and beat the waves against the
ever-tight'ning walls.

Demented, twisted, shattered: wonders
touched but never held

and Chaos rules. Waves retreat
and stumble, hesitate and

Die in scattered, rippled mem'ries of my
own belabored pulse.

Bed Is Too Small
79 – October 10-16, 2005

NON-FICTION – this is an excerpt from the book *North Country Quest*, which consists of stories about my hikes of the North Country Trail.

Wisconsin will be the first state in which I complete all the North Country Trail miles.

I'm totally psyched for this trip. Douglas County has recently decided that it will allow the trail to pass through county forests, which cover almost all of the western part of the state. I'll be connecting the Saint Louis River bridge at Jay Cooke State Park with the western boundary of the Chequamegon National Forest.

With over half of the trip being day hikes for which I'll spot myself by bicycle, I plan on making the most of the base camping opportunity. I'll cook my hot meals over a campfire and try a selection of new recipes. At home I hate to cook. Put me outside, make me light a fire and struggle with water and clean-up, and I'm suddenly transformed into a wannabe chef. Since it's October, I'm planning on hot breakfasts, complete with coffee. Menus include cheesy spuds, French toast, and hot grits and eggs. The evening meals include eggs and muffins cooked in orange halves, shrimp Creole, and Cascade stewpot. One of my evening meals turns out to be steaks, but I'm getting ahead of the story.

After deciding I don't like the lack of privacy and the amount of ATV traffic at a developed campsite, I tuck myself into a completely hidden space along the Black River. No one passing on the road can see my camp at all. Perfect. The only hitch is that the Douglas County Forest requires a permit for such dispersed camping. You are supposed to know which township and section you are camping in, and it has to be signed by a ranger. The price is extremely reasonable, but the logistics are impossible for hikers passing through on foot.

I'm sort of in luck. At least I have a car to get to the ranger station. However, the office is closed and I don't have the correct form. I write them a lengthy note, explaining my situation and detailing the problems with the requirement. I leave it and a check in a drop box and hope. They either never come looking for me, or they can't find me. So, I'll assume the best and guess that my explanation was good enough.

Douglas County is going to be the future host of many miles of gorgeous single-track trail, but their decision to allow the trail passage is recent, and most of these miles are not yet built. I've gotten a lot of information about places where I can leave the roadwalks to follow some flagged sections from Bill Menke. Wisconsin is where he lives, not just where he works, and he's always excited to help hikers who want to visit.

I organize a plan that allows me to ride the bike in the afternoons instead of the cold mornings. I'm so energized, I actually take a short bike ride after setting up my camp just because it will feel good before bedding down.

My camp side water source is not named the Black River for nothing. I realize that even filtered, this is going to be orange tannin tea, so I fill every lidded container I have in the car on my trip to town. When it's this easy to get better tasting water, do it!

In the morning, after French toast, and a wonderful discovery that slowly cooking the extra batter produces custard, I'm off to the St. Louis River at Jay Cooke State Park. This is slightly over the state line into Minnesota, but it's where I left off at the end of a previous hike.[1]

Today's miles take me across a broad valley alongside an active BNSF rail line. The sky is bright, the cows are pastured in

---

[1] See "Emily, Mama Rita, and Dick Have Their Way with the Regenwürmer," in *North Country Cache*.

October sunshine, and my fifteen-mile hike and twenty-mile bike ride are completed with plenty of daylight to spare. That energy level is holding strong. The temperate days sure help.

The single disappointment of the day is the eggs and biscuits cooked in orange shells. The rinds burn, and they don't hold enough food. Plan B is eggs plain, with scones made from the biscuit batter. Eat the oranges separately. Not such a gourmet presentation, but yummy.

I've decided to entertain myself in the evenings by practicing my ukulele. I'm not very good, but I struggle and sing my way through a notebook of favorite songs each night while I'm base camping. With the campfire's flames curling around the logs, dusk dropping its gauzy curtain, and a comforting hot drink to sip, I'm at peace. The first quarter moon shines so brightly it aspires to be full, even making moon shadows. However, I awake later to a steady rain which lasts the rest of the night. No matter how magical and mystical certain moments can be, there are always parts of an outdoor life that slam you back to reality.

Big Manitou Falls

The next day's miles include Pattison State Park. Pattison is the home of Big and Little Manitou Falls. The water is high and the falls are spectacular. I approach Big Manitou first, from the north. It's the highest falls in Wisconsin, at 165 feet. The drop is not sheer, but the water races down a rock sluiceway at a steep angle.

The Ojibwa called it Gitchee Manitou, or Great Spirit, because the sound of the water suggested the rumbling voice of a supreme being. At the south end of the park, Little Manitou is much shorter, at 30 feet; it is broad with a sheer drop. Both are impressive. The trail miles through the park are lovely but too few.

The Native American manitous and their animal spirits are strong on this hike. For the second time ever on the NCT, I see a Beaver instead of just evidence of its work. It waddles down the trail ahead of me leaving a broad tail track before slipping off into the woods. The beaver's spirit advice is to trust your creativity.

Two Great Horned Owls, atypically flying in the daytime, must have special meaning. Their spirit message is to have faith in the connection to the Source and in the ability to hear whispered messages from the Divine. One of them lights on a tree branch and watches me pass. Does he want to make sure I'm listening?

The bald eagle guides me to hold up my head with courage. A woodcock flies in front of me. Perhaps its meaning is freedom and health, universal messages ascribed to many birds. A fox suggests that the solution to any problem is at hand. The tiny and friendly Northern Redbelly Snake signifies transformation and a connection to the Life Force. I love watching him curl smoothly around my fingers as I return him to a natural environment instead of the road where he was so happy in the sun but flirting with mortal danger. Perhaps we are bestowing a transforming benediction on each other.

The next day I walk through a glacial outwash plain, much different from the northern forests. I also walk into a complete change of trail atmosphere.

The coarse soil in the outwash plain supports nutrient-poor pine barrens, preserved as Douglas County Wildlife Area. The 4000-acre sanctuary is characterized as a transitional savannah. Think open space with a few trees. It's maintained by fire for Sharp-tailed Grouse and other bird habitat and is now a bird sanctuary. The Wisconsin barrens are unique in that they also support prairie flowers and grasses.

What this means to the hiker is views and sunshine rather than being enclosed by trees while walking. The sun may be welcome or not, depending on the temperature of the day. However, there are only a few such ecosystems along the North Country Trail, and this one lends its ambiance to the diversity of trail experiences.

Bill Menke and his Roving Trail Crew have been building new trail through this section for the past week. I'm going to spend the night with them. I find the brand new treadway and perfectly painted blazes that lead me to the campsite where Bill has directed me. Despite arriving under sunny skies, earlier rain has guaranteed that all wood is wet. But I have a fire-building reputation to uphold.[2]

No one has arrived back at camp yet. Before anyone shows up, I have a cheerful blaze going, and Rolf, one of the regular trail builders, is more than happy to learn that he won't have to struggle with that chore.

Soon more guys from the crew arrive, and my solitary week is suddenly transformed into an evening with good friends, people who love the trail as much as I do, people who work hard with their hands and their resources to expand the off-road portions. I take a tour of the tool trailer, a workshop on wheels which can travel with them to any work site.

Now we've made it to the steaks. Dinner is straightforward and protein-packed. I probably wouldn't be able to eat my way through that big a piece of meat at this point in my life, but I certainly could that evening.

We spend the dusky hour around the fire, telling trail stories. They inform me I am the very first person (other than the builders) to walk the new piece of trail that leads into the campsite.

The following morning, two of the guys spot my car at the western end of the Chequamegon National Forest, the eastern end of this walk. I'll be backpacking the remainder of the miles I have planned through the Brule River State Forest. I'm hoping I have correctly sorted my gear, and have all the proper items for backpacking. No matter. My car is now gone, so whatever I have is what I will use. It's only two and a half days. I've become so accustomed to life on the trail that as long as I'm not missing

---

[2] See "She Who Builds Fire," in *North Country Cache*.

something as critical as sleeping bag or food or water bottles, anything else hardly makes a blip on the radar.

But I'm expecting great things from these few days, and they do not let me down. Before lunch I pass through the village of Solon Springs and a lovely county park. One more short roadwalk and I'm facing a hill that is one of my most anticipated climbs. I've been hearing about the next two-plus miles for over ten years.

This is an historic portage between the Bois Brule (usually just called Brule) and St. Croix Rivers. The Brule flows northward to Lake Superior in the Laurentian watershed. The St. Croix flows southward to the Mississippi, and Gulf of Mexico.

Bois Brule is French for "burnt wood," the meaning of the Ojibwa word for the place which was simply translated. Saint Croix is also French, for "holy cross," but this river's history is less clear. The Dakota and Ojibwe tribes spent over a century at war. Both had names for the waterway which had variations and ambiguous meanings. The earliest recorded name means "river of the grave," possibly because a native man who was bitten by a rattlesnake was buried there.

Somewhere along the Brule in 1842, the Ojibwe routed the Dakotas in battle, and the defeated tribe was pushed westward across the Mississippi.

Divides are fascinating and historically important places. While it's not on the NCT, there is a sign in Wisconsin at another place along this divide between the Laurentian and Mississippi Watersheds. Water falls from the sky, from a visually single cloud, but as the rain touches the earth some flows in one direction, and some the other. Two drops that descend as neighbors, and dissolve the same peaty chemicals from the same square inch of ground, will find destinations thousands of miles apart, determined by a chance landing. A puff of wind. A splash from a pine needle. A bird shaking its tail feathers.

The metaphysical aspects were unimportant to early travelers and explorers. What mattered to them was which waterways were large enough to float a canoe, and to then find two rivers or creeks from adjacent watersheds that were not far separated from each other. Here, a carry of under three miles up over a small hill was enough to connect a continuous passage between the St. Lawrence and Mississippi Rivers.

In 1933, the Daughters of the American Revolution, in an effort to preserve and interpret the important trail, placed boulders along the way, each bearing a plaque with the name of one well-known person who had used the portage.

As I climb the hill I pass "Nicholas, Jr. and Joseph Lucius 1886." Lucius was a member of one of the last expeditions to use this portage, as canals and railroads had captured commercial transportation. This expedition was led by Alexander McDougall, inventor of the whaleback boat, but Lucius was the one who recorded events. Nicholas was a postmaster at Solon Springs, a Civil War veteran who had escaped from the infamous Andersonville prison camp.

Next up on my walk from south to north, but previous in time, is "George R. Stuntz 1853." Stuntz was a government surveyor and wrote extensively about his work documenting the land for the newly approved state of Wisconsin.

The next stone is "Henry R. Schoolcraft 1820." Schoolcraft's name may be familiar to North Country Trail lovers. He extensively explored Michigan's Upper Peninsula and is credited with discovering the headwaters of the Mississippi at Lake Itasca. He commented in his journal that this was the "most practicable, easy, and expeditious water communication between the Mississippi River and Lake Superior."

"Jean Baptiste Cadotte 1819" is next (probably J.B. Cadotte II). He and his brother ran the American Fur Company and were partially responsible for making La Pointe on Madeline Island (in Lake Superior's Apostle Islands) a great trade center.

The following stone is "Michel Curot 1803." He wrote a journal of his passage with about twelve men to transport furs northward to Lake Superior shipping ports. This journal is entertaining, including everyday events, in addition to simple listings of provisions, times and dates. He mentions meeting with some Native Americans just north of the portage and receiving a fish and goose from them in exchange for credit to buy goods. He even includes their names, thus personalizing the visit.

"Jonathan Carver 1768" takes me a few steps farther back in time. He traveled westward from Fort Michilmackinac in

Michigan through Wisconsin to the Mississippi and wrote a journal of his adventures which became popular reading at the time. The British had recently won the territory from the French in the French and Indian War, and his was a journey of exploration. Perhaps we should credit him with following many miles of future North Country Trail.

First a Jesuit missionary, "Pierre LeSueur 1693," became a *coureur des bois,* an early trader of furs, pre-dating the Voyageurs, opening routes for the fur trade. Because of his knowledge of native languages he was involved in peace talks between the Ojibwe and the Dakotas, perhaps helping to hold that final war of 1842 at bay for a number of years.

Finally, I pass the stone of Daniel "Greysolon Delhut 1680," who is credited with discovering the portage. Of course he was shown the way by natives who had used the route for thousands of years before him. Duluth, Minnesota, is named for him.

The commemorative stones have a journey of their own to tell, not all of it a pleasant story, but the ending is one North Country Trail folks can be proud of. Sometime in the 1950s, vandals thought it would be fun to roll the stones down the steep bluff to the west of the portage trail. Decades of falling leaves, rainstorms and snows buried them from view. In 1990, Chuck Zosel of the Brule-St Croix Chapter of the North Country Trail Association began hunting for them. When I passed, only seven of the commemorative markers had been found and returned to their rightful places.

The eighth stone, the one for George Stuntz, had hidden deeper in the detritus and could not be located. In a most serendipitous occurrence, it was found just before the annual conference held in Ashland, Wisconsin, in 2010, so I was able to view all the stones in place on a group hike.

Although its use is now strictly recreational, vibrations from the ground of ancient moccasins and boots, the lingering scents of beaver pelts and gum to repair canoes, the sounds of arrows swishing through the air and the explosions of rifle fire are never far from a hiker's senses. Don't fail to stop and soak them in as you pass this way.

My goal for the night, my next-to-last night out on this trip, is the Jerseth Bluff Campsite high above the Bois Brule River. This is a fourteen-mile day in the full pack, but I'm so continually stimulated by the variety of experiences on this hike that I never become exhausted.

It's the sort of location I love—a flat spot with a great view across a valley, yet with lots of trees. I filter water and cook my dinner of St. Patrick's stew with coffee cake.

As evening falls, the moon, one day away from being full, rises to flood the woods with blue light. If I thought the first quarter was bright, this is astonishing. In truth, I later learn that the moon is only two days past perigee, the closest point on its orbit from earth. It's not my imagination. It really does appear brighter. The shadows of adjacent tree trunks on the tall white poplars create chiaroscuro stripes fading away from me to a vanishing point.

The night is also exceptionally clear and the stars are so bright they seem to perch, glittering, in the branches of balsam trees, reminding me of twinkling Christmas tree lights. Isn't it supposed to be the other way around? We put lights on an indoor evergreen to remind us of the stars and trees outside? But how many have lain on a hillside soaking in the beauty I find at Jerseth Bluff?

One of my favorite songs drifts through my consciousness, always true, but somehow quintessentially so tonight. (Except I'm not asking for the moon to be extinguished this time.)

> Bed is too small for my tiredness.
> Give me a hill topped with trees.
> Tuck a cloud up under my chin.
> Lord, blow the moon out, please.
> Rock me to sleep in a cradle of dreams.
> Sing me a lullaby of leaves.
> Tuck a cloud up under my chin.
> Lord, blow the moon out, please.[3]

The following day I stop for lunch on the rim of a bowl ringed with russet, gold, brown, and yellow aspen blazing in the sunshine. Scattered Jackpine dot the hollow. The spicy scent of

[3] "Bed is Too Small," by A. Farley, public domain.

Sweetfern rises to flavor my meal. Small flocks of Juncos and Chickadees entertain, playing hide and seek.

At Winneboujou campsite, I'm cheered by finding hard wood for my fire instead of stinky damp aspen.

On my final day I rest briefly at Morris Pond, another lovely place where one red tree on the far bank punctuates the gold.

Bill has warned me that there is a clearcut area I'll need to pass through almost at the end of my hike. In the middle of the logged section, at the top of a hill, is a memorial bench for Atley Oswald, a volunteer trail builder who has recently passed away. I sit to savor the last moments of my outing.

I was expecting a raw logged scar. Instead the opening is beginning to grow back, and I find it a high, lonely, beautiful kind of place. There are long views which are as satisfying as the embracing comfort of the forest. I record in my journal, "Well, a shower will feel good, but I'll miss the sun and the breeze and the quiet. I feel a strange mixture of wanting to be finished and yet not wanting it to end."

Suddenly there are tears in my eyes.

102 miles this hike
Jay Cooke State Park, MN to
Chequamegon National Forest, WI
Carlton County, MN
Douglas and Bayfield Counties, WI
2895 total NCT miles

Dream Dance

Deep green sweep of hemlock bough,
cradle of my dreams tonight, And now

barred owl starts his query, "who,
who... who cooks for you?"

Blue-black roof, velvet, high,
impaled by troupes of pin-point fire

arc-ing, marking my drooping lids.
Ignite a spark within, and bid

me rise, see dreams. Soul dance,
flame-led, I leap in sleep, entranced.

Wild, the child, this sprite within
dances her night-time, dream-time whim

Till dawn stills the whirling play.
Exhausted, filled, I greet the day.

Why I Hate Cell Phones

HUMOR

Don't get me wrong; I have no problem with technology. In fact, when I can afford new techie toys, I embrace them.

The problem is that my cell phone is more organic than electronically organized. It tends to leap like an incautious frog into the depths of the couch, or slither underneath a pile of papers on my desk. When I walk to the mailbox, that sneaky little creature, disguised as a rectangle of metal and plastic, manages to wriggle out of my pocket and find a perch on the retaining wall, from which to enjoy the afternoon breezes. Is it catching flies?

So it's sneaky. Maybe I could live with that. But I'm here to tell you that it has become downright nasty of late. It hides my messages. Seriously. After an expedition yesterday to locate the wayward beast I peered between its grinning lips and was rewarded with the information that I had two new messages. I pushed the button that is supposed to let me "listen now." Nothing.

I slapped the gaping rictus closed, and with a flounce of irritation nearly tossed the critter back in the pond. Then I remembered, "press 1." OK, I can do that. I pressed 1 and called voicemail. "You have no new messages," I was informed in a hollow voice.

Great, that's just great. This annoying beast speaks with a forked tongue. Do I have two messages, or no messages? Based on past experience, I'm pretty sure that I do have messages, but they will not be regurgitated for me to listen to for at least two days. If someone really needs me to respond soon, too bad.

Then there is the problem of how to maintain this wayward pet. It demands feeding every day or it goes into hibernation. It refuses to be cuddled affectionately between shoulder and ear the way its predecessor enjoyed. No, it insists on being held by at least one hand. Even its voice is unpleasant. Unless fed extra greens it insists on singing snatches of horrid pop songs instead of croaking a simple "Ring-it!"

Just one more little push, one more swallowed message, another game of hide and seek, and you'll find me sending this monster back to the mud and keeping a pocket frog instead. I think we'll get along better.

Apple Tree

The gnarled apple that held the treehouse came
down today tumbling ghosts of small boys
holding hammers and a can full of rusted nails.

When did you become decrepit?

Wrinkled arms covered with blossoms, no fruit

Where have you gone, my sons?

Gray

Tone-deaf ear,
Shrouded fear.

Pin-stripe suit,
Unknown fruit.

Dawn-mist deer
Pain-drowned tear.

Not there nor here–
Not absolute.

The Case of the Cautious Couple

MYSTERY SPOOF – This short story won first place in the Accentuate Writers contest on the theme of "engagement." Readers of the Perry Mason books will quickly recognize the formula, despite the changing of names. It was previously published in *Short and Fun Stories*, Volume 1, by Mercer Publications.

1

The light tripping of heels in the hallway sounded confident, but just outside the frosted glass door the steady tattoo became hesitant and then halted. Stella Deet looked up from her typing and waited, assessing the visitor even before the door was opened. When the tentative knock came, Stella rose and opened the door to admit a well-dressed young woman, who smiled nervously and walked toward the secretary.

"I'd like to speak with Mr. Berry Grayson," she began, lifting her chin. "My name is Ima Basquette Case."

"May I tell Mr. Grayson the nature of your problem," Stella countered.

"No... yes... it's about my fiancé. He's being cautious, and I'm worried."

Stella Deet raised an eyebrow and entered Grayson's private office. "Whom do we have in the waiting room this morning?" Grayson greeted his confidential assistant warmly.

"A Miss Ima Basquette Case, boss. She's usually sure of herself, and gets what she goes after. Upper middle class, a working girl, probably in a private office–nice suit classed up with a small fur and new shoes. But she dressed in a hurry, and she's engaged but has no ring."

Now it was Grayson's turn to raise an eyebrow. "All that in

ten seconds, Stella?" he asked.

Stella smiled enigmatically. "I have to earn my salary, Chief."

Grayson stared calmly at Stella till she lowered her eyes and replied, "Oh, all right. Her slip is showing"

"What seems to be your problem, Miss Case?" Grayson asked, after escorting the young woman into his office, and glancing toward the hem of her skirt to verify Stella's assertion.

"Thank you for seeing me, Mr. Grayson. Frankly, I don't know who else to turn to. Have you heard of Loden A. Gunn?"

"As in Gunn Investments?"

"Yes, that's the one.

"Well?"

"I'm engaged to his son. At least, I think I am." Her right hand nervously fluttered to her left ring finger. "Let me be frank with you. I have been previously married to a Mr. Case. I was young and he was rather an empty personality, as it turned out. He left me soon after the wedding and we filed for divorce. I have those papers with me. I don't think that this is the source of the problem." She fished an envelope from her purse and thrust it at the attorney. He nodded toward his secretary and the girl surrendered the papers to Stella.

"My fiancé's name is Schott."

"Schott Gunn?"

"Yes, that's right, Mr. Grayson. Do you know him as well as his father?"

"We may have met in relation to an earlier case."

"Oh, then you know my ex-husband, too"

"No, I don't believe so. Why do you ask?'

"You just mentioned him, my ex, Early R. Case."

"Why don't we confine our discussion to this case, uh... problem, Mrs. Case?"

"As you wish, Mr. Grayson. Call me Miss Case. Anyway, everything was going along fine until last week. We needed to get the marriage license and had an appointment all set. Then Schott called and cancelled. I didn't think much about it, and simply called the courthouse to re-schedule. When I gave Schott the new date, he said he didn't think he could make that either. Since then, I've telephoned him every day, and he simply won't take my calls."

"Why do you think this is a case for a lawyer?" Grayson asked. "After all, many men have second thoughts and prefer to avoid a confrontation rather than to simply be honest."

"It's just not like Schott at all!" Ima protested, turning to Stella. "Oh, Miss Dreet, you're a woman. You have to see how it is. We are like two peas in a pod. We chose my engagement ring together, and it's just waiting to be picked up at the jewelers. He's kind and caring and enjoys my company. He's not in love with having a wife; he's in love with me. Don't you see? He's everything that Early R. wasn't. I can't let him go without a fight. I don't know what has made him so cautious all of a sudden."

Grayson looked at Stella and she gave an imperceptible nod of her head.

"All right, Ima." We'll look into it, but it may turn out to be nothing at all."

"Oh, thank you, Mr. Grayson! I'm perfectly willing to pay for your help. I've saved two hundred dollars from my salary. Will that be enough to retain you?"

"We'll invest that into finding out what's bothering your fiancé, and perhaps it won't even cost that much."

2

When the young woman had left his office, Grayson sighed and dialed the phone. "How you talk me into these routine little cases, Stella, I'll never understand. This one is sure to be quite boring."

"I understand, Chief, but she was so earnest and optimistic, I just hate to see her hopes dashed."

Grayson, with the phone to his ear, smiled quietly at his assistant and then spoke, "Saul? Berry here. I have a routine matter I'd like you to run down for me. It shouldn't take more than a few hours."

Saul Frake, the long-limbed and longsuffering detective who worked regularly for Grayson, replied, "Sure, Berry. But I know better than to think that any job you send my way is ordinary. What's the scoop?"

"Check on Loden Gunn, of Gunn Investments. He's got a son, Schott, who has suddenly become shy of a marriage proposal he's made to a young lady. Find out about the family. Look for another girl friend or some scandal, but don't spend over a hundred dollars."

"Gunn's shy?"

"Yes."

"What's the girl's name?

"Ima Basquette Case."

"Berry, it's that girl that should be shy."

"Why's that Saul?"

"She's headed for a lifetime as Ima Gunn."

3

The next morning Berry Grayson strode purposefully into his office and with a deft flick of the wrist snapped his hat onto the bust of Blackstone which rested in the corner of the tastefully arranged office. Stella Deet looked up from her typing and smiled. "I'll pick it up in a minute, Chief," she offered.

"Why, Stella, whatever has gotten into you this morning? You aren't supposed to say things like that."

"Gee, Chief, don't you think it's time we started telling readers the truth? It's giving me cramps in my fingers to keep banging out these tortured reports."

"What do you mean, Stella? Truth is my middle name."

"Here we've been, doing these same things for thirty years and we've never aged a bit. Someone is eventually going to figure out that sometimes you miss that toss."

"Can it, Stella! Readers don't want to hear that part. Get on the phone and call up Mr. Schott Gunn. Get him in here, and let's simply ask him his side of the story."

"Will do!" Her fingers deftly twirled the dial and in a few minutes she reported that Mr. Gunn was exceedingly busy this morning due to a death in the family, but that he would be more than happy to stop in for a few minutes around ten a.m. He knew that Ima was worried, and wanted to clear things up.

At nine-fifty the phone rang, and Stella scooped the receiver to her ear. "Hi, Stella! Is the boss around? I've got some news on that Case case."

"Right here, Saul. I'll put him on." She plugged in the line to Grayson's private office, and he joined the conversation.

"Here's the deal, Berry. Schott Gunn's parents are Loden A. and Stealla Gunn. Loden's father is Thomas, usually referred to as Tommy. He supposedly made a pile of money in lead mining back in the nineteen-oughts. Now here's where I think young Schott has found his sticking point. I can't find any record of his parents' marriage. Your boy may be illegitimate. He probably just found out about it himself. Let me come down to your office and I'll show you the family history."

"Come ahead, Saul. I think you've probably put your finger on the problem."

Grayson and Stella Deet hung up their phones and listened for Saul's steps in the corridor. Instead, they heard the tapping of feminine heels, and Ima Case entered the outer office.

"Mrs... Miss Case, come in. Let me take your coat," Stella offered. "Mr. Frake, our detective, is just coming in with some information that I think will answer your questions."

"Thank you, Miss Street, but I have some terrible news. I just know Schott is going to need me, but I'm afraid that he's become too cautious to admit it."

Just then Frake's code knock sounded on the door and the detective stepped into the group. "Sorry, Berry, I thought you were alone."

"No problem, Saul. Meet Ima Case. It's her case you are on, er... her situation you've been looking into. Tell us what you've got."

"O.K., Berry." The detective rolled out some notarized copies of documents, placed them on the desk and weighted the corners with various objects.

"But, everything has changed now!" protested Ima. "Thomas, Schott's grandfather, died last night. Everyone says he's worth a fortune, but no one knows for sure until the will is read. I don't want him to think I'm a gold-digger. I simply have to get Schott to talk to me!"

"Calm down, young lady," ordered the lawyer. "This is all part of the picture. It may be helpful. You can add any details you might know."

Frake smoothed out a chart, apparently copied from a family Bible. "I got this from the cemetery records. Someone was really interested in documenting the Gunn family plot a few years ago. Here's what it shows. Thomas Gunn was married to Carrie Theball in 1909. Their son, Loden was born in 1911. This line shows a union for Loden Gunn with Stealla Bundle, but there's no date. Then on September 20, 1938, Schott was born. Does that sound right, Miss Case?"

"Oh, yes, that's Schott's birth date," replied Ima.

"O.K., then that seems to check. But there are two things that are funny about this. I went by the courthouse, and there is no record of Loden and Stealla ever being married. Sometimes paperwork gets, lost, Berry, but the union would probably have been somewhere between 1929 and 1937, and the records for those years are really in order—no fires or floods–and there's just nothing. Of course Loden might have married before he was eighteen; I can do some more digging."

"What's the other odd thing, Saul?"

"Well, look here." Frake pointed to the top of the chart. Ima edged closer in order to see better and picked up the paperweight which was obscuring that corner of the document. "There's another line connecting Tommy, Thomas, with a woman named Violet. But there is no last name given, just the initial B. And it looks like someone started to write the name of her son or daughter and then tried to blot it out. You can just see what might be the letters A-s, and then it's all a mess." I saw the original, and you can't tell anything from it either.

Suddenly the paperweight fell to the floor with a loud crack. Everyone's eyes turned to Ima, who was pale and trembling. "Get her in a chair, Stella. She's going to faint." cried Grayson.

"No, no, I'm fine," Ima protested. I... I didn't eat any breakfast, and this is all very stressful. I will just sit down for a moment, if you don't mind." She lowered herself into the chair that Stella brought, leaned over to pick up the paperweight and composed herself. "Really, I'm sorry to be so silly. It's nothing. Please go on."

Frake looked at the lawyer, who nodded, and he continued. "No one seems to know who this Violet is. Without a last name it's going to be a little hard to track that down, and I didn't know how much it mattered anyway, since Schott is certainly Loden's son. Give me some more time and I can..."

Just then there came another knock on the door, a firm and crisp rapping of manly knuckles. Grayson turned the knob to admit a thin, but athletic looking young man wearing a modest, yet classic, suit of fine wool flannel. His blond hair was trimmed neatly and he held his hat in his hand, but his eyes were bloodshot and his complexion was slightly gray. "Ima!" he exclaimed immediately, taking in the group at the desk. "You are just the person that I've been looking for."

Miss Case's eyes flitted nervously from the newcomer to Grayson.

"Excuse me, I'm Schott Gunn," the young man brought his voice down a notch and held out his hand to Grayson. "You're Berry Grayson. I've seen your picture in the paper."

"Hello, Mr. Gunn. You might as well be part of all this. Meet Saul Frake, a detective, and this is Stella Deet, my assistant."

"Pleased to meet you," he nodded to each and then plunged back into his original mood. "Ima, I'm so sorry that I haven't been taking your calls. It's just that, well, when I asked Mom and Pops about getting my birth certificate for the marriage license, Mom got really cagey. We played cat and mouse with words for a couple of days, and then I finally got her to tell me... she and Pops were never married. She said it didn't seem to matter much at first. Then Pops got into this investment business, and he started to stand out in his social set. They went to parties and all, were even in the paper some. Mom said that she couldn't bear the idea of the embarrassment it would cause if they tried to back up and get married then, after living together for several years already. So they just never did. Anyway, you can imagine how that made me feel for a few days. I'll tell you, I was pretty shocked. Here I am, the son of an investment banker, and the grandson of the famous Tommy Gunn..." he paused and ducked his head. "But then I got to thinking... it's a new age. Nobody cares about the old conventions. After all, it's not my fault my folks don't have a piece of paper. Let's get out of this stuffy office and go pick up your engagement ring."

Ima continued to nervously finger the paperweight. "What about your grandfather, Schott?" she asked.

"Yeah, he died last night. Let me tell you, there's a lot of turmoil going on over at my house right now. But it will sort itself out. I have to be at the offices of Grindstone and Upthecreek at three o'clock for the reading of the will, but we're free till then. All that talk about his fortune is just a bunch of family myths anyway. He was a nice old guy who had something of a reputation back in Galena, Illinois at those lead mines because he had a tough name, but after all, he died with two suits in his closet and a rusty Packard in the driveway. How much could he be worth?"

All eyes turned to Ima Case. She seemed to shrink under their collective gaze. "I think you had better spend the time with your family today, Schott," she said coolly. I'll be in touch after the funeral." Quickly retrieving her coat, the young woman practically bolted for the door.

"Well, she's probably right, at that," Schott grinned good-naturedly. "Say, thanks for everything! I was a fool to almost lose her over a silly piece of paper. I'll pay your bill, Mr. Grayson. I bet she gave you cash from her savings account. She's quite the girl, and I'm going to do right by her, just as soon as this thing with my grandfather is sorted out." Almost as abruptly as the girl, Gunn left the office.

Grayson, Saul and Stella were left shaking their heads, still holding down the edges of the family tree document. "Well, I guess that's all there is to it, Berry," said Saul. "I suppose there's no sense pursuing this any farther."

"That's right, Saul. It looks like a happy ending."

"Not so fast, boys!" Stella piped up. "Don't you see? We've still got a cautious couple, only now Ima's the one who has cold feet. You saw her practically run out of here. You can't stop now."

"Gosh, Berry, I guess she's right. Something spooked that girl. What were we doing when she got all shaky?"

"It was when she saw this side of the chart, where Violet

is," said Stella.

Grayson noted the look of a woman in love with young lovers in his secretary's eye, and with a chuckle said, "O.K., Saul. We can spend a little more on this. Get busy finding out about this shrinking Violet."

4

Two days later, Grayson was relaxing in his apartment and thinking about going to bed. The clock struck eleven, and he folded the paper he had been reading. The big news in the city was indeed that of Tommy Gunn's will. The bequests seemed ordinary enough. His estate was to be divided equally among all living heirs. The problem was, what and where was the estate? Gunn's will stated that the bulk of the legacy was left in the safekeeping of one James Baines. But that name was unknown to anyone in the family. Reporters had blown the story into a half-page spread.

Unexpectedly the phone rang. That number was known only to Saul Frake and Stella Deet. Grayson leaped from his chair and answered just as the second ring began. "Berry, you better get down here fast." It was Frake. "Gunnildr Gunn has just been shot. Lt. Bragg is hopping mad– he's sure you're involved somehow in this..."

"Slow down, Saul. Who is this person, Gunn.. Gunn?"

"Gunnildr. She's Loden's unmarried sister. It's some old Norwegian name that means gun. She was poking around in Tommy's back yard and someone blasted her with a shotgun. Schott Gunn found her and called the police. She's a goner. They haven't found the shooter or the shotgun, but the neighbors heard the gunshot. Schott came by thinking that he'd spend some time looking through his grandfather's house to see if he could find whatever it is the old coot left them all and found Gunnildr dead in the driveway."

"I think I've got you, Saul. I'll be there as soon as I pick up Stella. You're at the Thomas Gunn house?"

"Right."

Thirty minutes later Grayson's coupe pulled into the end of

the long driveway at the crime scene. In the headlights, Bragg paced back and forth. Berry Grayson and Stella Deet emerged from the car and approached the police lieutenant. "I hear you're looking for me, Bragg."

"That's right, Grayson. You've put your foot in it this time. We've got Schott Gunn."

"You found the weapon?"

"No, we've got the murderer. It's pretty obvious. Schott already found the inheritance, and he's now trying to narrow the field of people he has to share it with. He shot his aunt, ditched the shotgun and returned just in time to "discover" the body. We've got his bloody shoes, and his hands are covered in gun oil. He's only said two words since we cuffed him."

"What are they, Bragg?"

"'Berry Grayson.'"

5

Stella Deet observed, "Here comes Saul, Chief."

"Berry, I have to say that it looks pretty bad for young Gunn."

"Tell me about it, Saul."

"Well, he did report the body. That's in his favor. But step over here. I've been trying to poke around a little bit out of the view of that guard near the body. He won't give me the time of day. Now, it looks very much as if the shooter was over here by this old Packard. Watch it! The police haven't noticed this yet, but let's not make a mess–this might be important, but I don't have a clue what it means just yet.

"All right, Saul, get to the point."

"It's your nickel, Berry! See the crushed grass on this side of the car? It sure looks like someone walked over here from those woods and used the car for cover. I didn't dare turn on a flashlight and attract attention but it looks to me like the black paint on the hood right here has been roughed up in a line– almost like someone was resting the barrel of a gun here. And right over there... careful... don't let that guard see you looking... is the shotgun shell. It's yellow and stands out like a sore thumb.

I can't figure out why the police haven't been looking over here at all. Now here's the next thing. Take a look at the bumper. You can see that the edge of it is all smeared with oil. It looks like someone cleaned the gun and spilled oil all over the bumper, there where it's shiny. Schott Gunn was covered with gun oil; you could smell him a mile away, Berry."

Flashlights stabbed through the darkness and Lt. Bragg's voice snapped with authority. "Over here, men!" Addressing the group huddled around the old car he ordered peremptorily, "Get away from that car, you three! Now I get really suspicious, Berry, when I see you contentedly snooping around far away from the body."

"We hardly have a choice, Bragg. You've got the entire crime scene well protected."

"Yes, well, let's just put some light on this scene, Grayson. I knew it! Here's a shotgun shell. Bag this up, boys. Watch where you are walking, now."

"Find something interesting, Bragg?"

"Berry, I have half a mind to accuse you of throwing this shell into the grass yourself, but until I can prove it, we'll assume it's from the murder weapon. Now, I want you folks out of here, pronto. I mean gone, get in your cars and leave, gone. Don't tempt me to find a reason to really detain you."

6

Not long afterwards the three co-workers were seated in a comfortable booth at the Schooner's Rail, a neighborhood grill, enjoying dessert and coffee. Frake and Grayson were forking into steaming slabs of apple pie a la mode, and Stella had let herself be talked into a small slice of lemon meringue. Grayson's hand wandered across the seat and covered Stella's affectionately while they sipped their coffee.

"The thing just doesn't make sense, Saul. If Schott is guilty, of course he would ditch the gun before reporting the body. But he can't be stupid enough to get rid of the weapon yet overlook the spent shell."

"What I don't understand is the oil," Stella contributed.

"Did you notice Schott's clothes?" The men shook their heads. "He was dressed in work pants and a flannel shirt with a big tear in the sleeve. You saw him at the office, Berry. That's not his usual appearance. He's almost a clothes horse. He went there expecting to do something that would be really dirty. He wouldn't need to dress like that just to shoot someone."

"She's right, Berry," added Frake. "The whole thing is goofy. If you plan to kill someone you don't wait till you are facing your victim to clean your gun. I wonder what else the police have, because Schott Gunn has to be innocent."

The beefy owner of the restaurant was approaching the table with the coffee pot. He arrived just in time to hear the final sentence of the detective's speech.

"You folks followin' that Gunn case? I read all about it in the papers. Ain't that somethin' with that crazy old Tommy Gunn guy leavin' his life savings on a ship?" The man chuckled heartily.

"It's quite remarkable," commented Grayson, winking at Stella out of sight of the man with the coffee pot.

"Tell us how you figured it out," asked Stella demurely, smiling up at the big man. "It's always fascinating to hear the different ways that people solve such sophisticated puzzles."

"Oh, shucks, Miss. 'T'weren't nothin'. Look around the room." The trio raised their eyes to the walls which were covered with paintings and prints of oceangoing, full-rigged sailing ships.

"And James Baines is connected with one of these vessels?" Stella continued.

"Oh, you're just putting me on, now," said the man. "You know that one over there," he pointed to a black schooner, with gilded trim, sailing over very blue waves, "is the James Baines. Fastest clipper ship that ever sailed! Set an Atlantic record of twelve-and-a-quarter days from Boston to Liverpool, England. Then she sailed around the world and, by gum, she set another record! One-hundred thirty-three days, no joke."

"Where is that ship now?" queried Frake.

"She burned to the waterline in 1858;" he shook his head mournfully. "Just three days after the insurance expired. Converted to a coal barge, and finally ended up as a floating dock. Sad end for the fastest of the old clippers.

"You ready for some more joe?" he added, lifting the pot, suddenly sheepish about his long speech.

After their cups were re-filled and the sail enthusiast returned to the kitchen, the discussion continued about the James Baines. "So Thomas hid his fortune on some obscure dock in England?" Frake asked, shaking his head in confusion.

Grayson's eyes were shining." I think the solution is much closer to home Saul. Haven't we seen a black Clipper lately?"

"With gilded trim!" Stella chipped in, the excitement mounting in her voice.

Frake's eyes widened. "I'll be dog-goned," he exclaimed.

7

Grayson sat at the table across from Schott Gunn in the visitor's room at the jail. "Keep your voice low," he warned.

"Mr. Grayson, I haven't got a clue what's going on. I went to my grandfather's house, because I was pretty sure that I knew where his treasure was."

"And did you find it?"

"I think so!" the young man's voice rose in eagerness.

"Keep it down," warned Grayson.

"Well, he was just crazy about that car of his. So I could never figure out why he let it sit out in the weather and rust. That car was a 1942 Packard Clipper. He had it customized with fake gold-plated trim to make it look like those real gold-trimmed speedsters. I'd been in his house a lot, so I knew there wasn't much there but a bunch of junk. But I got the idea that maybe he'd hid a stash of money in that car somehow. So I took some gun oil to loosen the rusted bolts and a wrench. I decided I'd take it apart piece by piece if I had to."

"After dark? That looks like you were trying to hide something."

"I went after dark because I didn't figure there was any reason to call attention to what I was doing until I had some real information. So I got there about ten-thirty, and I started to clean off some of the grime on the old Clipper. I rubbed that bumper down with gun oil, and you know what, Mr. Grayson?"

"What, Schott?"

"That crazy old Tommy was crazy like a fox! We all thought that car trim was gold-painted chrome. But it's the real thing, pure gold. He'd smeared mud around to keep it looking like an old junker and left it out in the rain because he knew that real gold wouldn't corrode. I guess he really did turn lead into gold!"

"So, you found the inheritance, but what about your aunt? After all, Schott, that's the reason you are here."

"Oh, they'll let me out soon. Gosh, Mr. Grayson, I didn't do anything."

"That's not exactly what the police think."

Gunn gave Grayson one of those impossibly optimistic looks of the very young. "Well, anyway, when I got to fooling around with that bumper, pretty soon I saw a fresh shotgun shell in the grass, and a scratch in the hood of the car. It looked like the gun had been pointed back toward the curve in the driveway, so I went to investigate. I found Aunt Gunny, Gunnildr. We all called her Gunny. It was a mess, I can tell you that. I never saw anything like that before. I probably don't sound like I care very much, but the family hardly ever saw her. She came for the funeral, and I guess she was still around. I don't know why she was at my grandfather's house. Anyway, I ran in the house and called the police. You pretty much know the rest."

"Where are the wrench and the gun oil?"

"Probably on the kitchen table, with a couple of rags, where I left them when I phoned."

"What have you told the police?"

"Nothing at all. You may think I'm just a kid, Mr. Grayson, but my Pops taught me how to keep my mouth shut and wait. I'll wait till you tell me what to say."

"All right, Schott, you may be smart enough, at that."

"Can you do me one favor, Mr. Grayson?"

"What's that?"

"I'm really worried about Ima. I haven't heard from her at all since she left your office. I've been calling and driving past her house, well, until they stuck me in here, and she's just disappeared. I guess maybe she thinks I'm not good enough for her now, but I wish she'd say it to my face. If I could only have another chance to convince her that I love her..." his voice broke.

"I'll try to find her, Mr. Gunn. You're sure you can sit tight?"

The young man grinned. "I'm not going far," he answered.

8

Grayson latchkeyed the door to his private office. He could hear Stella Deet already pounding away at the typewriter as he entered. "Come in here, Stella," the lawyer called.

"What's up, Chief?" Stella asked, coming around the corner.

"I guess we've found the treasure, but we've still got a mystery. I need your help."

"Saul called a little while ago. That car has been tentatively appraised at over $100,000. It will be a couple of days before they get it disassembled and know the exact weight of the gold. But what other mystery are you hiding?"

"Schott made me promise to look up Ima Case. No one seems to know where she is. I thought you might have some ideas."

"Ah, the other half of the cautious couple! I forgot to ask Saul if he found out anything about the Violet that made our young lady shrink. I've been racking my brain; she sure seemed convinced that Schott was the perfect catch, and then..." The phone rang stridently, and Stella paused to answer. "Berry Grayson's office. Who's calling please?"

The transmitter emitted squawking noises. "Miss Case, won't you please speak to Mr. Grayson," Stella implored, but the connection was broken.

Grayson raised his eyebrows. "Miss Ima Case?"

"Yes, she asked us to deliver a message to Schott Gunn. She says there will be no wedding, and that she is now seeing a man named Robert Akesall. Schott is not to contact her again."

"Nothing else?"

"She hung up on me, Chief! This is just too sudden. I know there is something wrong, something really deep that's bothering her. We have to get to the bottom of it all! Young love is so excruciating; it's a wonder that any lovers under the age of twenty-five ever make it to the altar. Now, take people our age as an example of the opposite. We know what we want, and who we are comfortable with. We've lived with ourselves through enough crises and hard times to know how we'll react. So when someone we care about acts strangely we don't go running off second-guessing that person and our own feelings. I guess that's love, Chief!"

"Stella! You haven't talked about love since that cruise to Hawaii."

"Oh yes, the one where a jury-tamperer staged his own murder and escaped by disguising himself as a man with a broken neck?"

"Yes, and the one where I proposed to you in the moonlight."

"Chief, it's just no use. Sure, we are comfortable together. But I don't want to be stuck in some house waiting for you to show up after you've solved a case. We work together. Besides, you'd lose half your readers. Women do read about your cases, Mr. Berry Grayson!"

"What about an engagement, Stella? We could stay perpetually engaged, and then I could tell you that I love you."

"I suppose it wouldn't be any more silly than staying the same age for all these years. But, no. Not today, anyway. We've got work to do!"

9

At exactly nine-forty-seven the next morning, Schott Gunn was being escorted from the jail to the county courthouse for a preliminary hearing. The two buildings were not far separated, and low-risk prisoners were often walked the half-block, secured with handcuffs and leg irons. As Gunn and the deputy passed the alley mid-block, a blast echoed between the brick buildings. Blood appeared along Gunn's left side and began to seep into the fabric of his prison uniform. The young man staggered against the deputy and fell heavily to the pavement. Footsteps retreated from the far end of the alley. The deputy hesitated, not knowing whether to leave the prisoner to pursue the apparent shooter, or stay at his duty post. He stayed. Gunn's wounds appeared to be messy, but not life-threatening.

Within a few minutes the wail of an ambulance was heard; and the injured man was soon transported to the nearest hospital. Grayson, waiting in the courtroom, was as surprised as anyone when the bailiff appeared and reported what had occurred, "He's been taken to Memorial Center."

Berry Grayson returned to his office and explained to Stella Deet what had happened. "Call the hospital, Stella. Find out how he is."

In short order, Stella had convinced the emergency room personnel that Gunn had a right to see his lawyer as soon as possible. But she was told that he was still in surgery, and wouldn't be fit to talk with anyone for a few hours at the earliest.

"Stella, we've just got to look at this whole situation a different way now. Someone has killed Tommy Gunn's daughter, and now there's an attempt on the life of his grandson. That should tell us something."

"And both crimes were committed with a shotgun, Chief. That's what the nurse told me—that they were removing shot from Schott's side. Fortunately the gunman was a little too far away. He's going to have a lot of nasty wounds to heal, but no major organs were damaged."

"Hang it, Stella, I can't just sit here. Let's go visit Loden A. Gunn, and see what he knows about all this."

10

Dejectedly, Grayson and Stella Deet walked down the hospital corridor toward room three-twelve, where they had been directed. Their interview with Loden Gunn had been unproductive. "He must be keeping something from us, Stella," Grayson said impatiently. "No one could be that ignorant of his own family."

"Don't be so sure, Chief. Loden has been hiding behind piles of money for his adult life, and he probably didn't really want to know more about his father's past.

"Well, here we are. Let's see if Schott has any idea who

might have done this."

The couple nodded to the guard outside the door marked 312, and entered the room to find the handsome young man lying in bed reading a magazine. At first glance he looked as if nothing was amiss, but as they approached the bed it became obvious that his left side was a patchwork of sterile gauze pads and adhesive tape. Schott grinned.

"Mr. Grayson!" Boy, am I glad to see you! Those coppers have sure changed their tune. Now they are guarding me for my protection, not to keep me from escaping. I guess getting shot is one way to prove your innocence!"

"How are you feeling?" asked Stella.

"Oh, I'm going to be plenty sore for a week or so. And I guess I'll have one scar that will show on this side of my face." He turned so they could see the bandage. "I'm going to pretend it gives me character," Schott concluded. "Have you found Ima?"

"No, and we'd like to ask you more about her," Grayson steered the conversation to the young woman. "What do you know about her family?"

"Well, she was raised by her father after her mother died. They came from Illinois. That's sort of how we got acquainted. I met her at a party her boss gave for some of his clients, and we joked about both having relatives from back East. But she didn't seem to want to talk about her childhood, and I didn't press her. I won't let her future be unhappy, so the past didn't seem to matter very much."

"So her father's last name is Basquette? That's her maiden name"

"I guess so, Mr. Grayson. Does it matter?"

"Perhaps," the lawyer mused.

11

By four p.m., Saul Frake was seated crosswise in the overstuffed chair of Grayson's office. He was bursting with news, but only his closest friends would have been able to tell. His sleepy countenance and relaxed posture were his greatest assets in protecting his profession from detection. "I think I've figured out who Violet B. might be," he began.

"We're all ears," encouraged Stella.

"As I said, without a last name I was pretty much working in the dark. But I figured that we have one person connected to this case whose initial is B. That's Ima Case, nee Basquette. So I went hunting for a Violet Basquette, and sure enough, there is one. Now I haven't found out about her exactly, but she appears on the death certificate of a young woman named Charity Basquette, as the one who reported the death. Charity was married to her son Ashley, and died giving birth to a girl named Ima."

"Oh, Saul!" cried Stella. "No wonder Ima nearly fainted and has been acting so strangely. She's Schott's cousin!"

"It looks like it, Stella," agreed Frake.

"She recognized the problem the minute she saw that family tree," added Grayson.

"There's more, Berry."

"More? All right, Saul, let's hear it."

"Once I had that name, I started backtracking. Her address was listed as Galena, Illinois, and that all fit, of course, since we knew that's where Tommy made all his money. I called a partner agency in Illinois, and had them nose around. It seems that Tommy was quite the playboy. He was married to Carrie, like we said the other day. But my colleagues started interviewing some of the old-timers, and they were more than eager to share some fifty-year-old dirt. Tommy and Violet were seen together more than might have been considered appropriate, but the real scandal was a lady named Dahlia. He had known her long before he met Carrie, and it seems he never got over her. One old guy swears that his sister owned a rooming house where this Dahlia stayed, and that the word on the sly was that the bills were paid by none other than Tommy Gunn."

"So what, Saul? How does that bear on our young lady's case?"

"Darned if I know, boss. I'm just tracking down leads. But this same fellow did mention that it was fresh on his mind because someone else has been asking pretty much the same questions, only a few days before we got there."

Grayson raised his eyebrows, and simultaneously, the phone rang. Stella answered and in a few moments replaced the receiver and reached for her purse. "Get your hats, boys. We've been summoned by Schott Gunn. He has a visitor."

As the trio approached the elevator, the door opened and Lt. Bragg advanced toward them. "We've got the gun, Berry," he began. "Some old lady over on Applewood Avenue went out to add some fish guts to her trash can and found a sawed-off shotgun. It had one shell in it, same make and shot size as the casing from Tommy's driveway. No prints. Thought I'd see what you had to say about it." He paused. "You folks seem to be going somewhere in a hurry."

"Tag along, Bragg, we're headed for some answers."

As they entered the elevator, Frake leaned over and whispered a name in Grayson's ear.

12

Lt. Bragg nodded to the guard outside room 312. A nurse approached authoritatively as if to protest this large number of visitors to one room, but the steely stares of the hard-boiled lieutenant and resolute lawyer stopped her in her tracks.

But not one of them was prepared for the sight inside the hospital room. A sprightly lady of about eighty years of age was perched on a chair beside Schott Gunn, who was looking tired but determined. The woman's hair was blued, but still thick and curled attractively around her wrinkled face. She wore a magenta suit with a purple belt, and a woven, matching purse was tucked under the chair. Gunn grinned and pulled himself up higher in the bed. Meet "Violet Basquette," he announced wryly. "She's been bringing me up to date on the family history."

"Pleased to make your acquaintance," began Miss Basquette, after everyone had been introduced. "Perhaps I should tell the story again."

"We'd be delighted," answered Stella.

"See, I'm from Illinois. Galena, to be exact. The same as Schott's granddad. I was the owner of the Lead Pants Saloon. Pretty good living for a girl like me. I never was one to be very demure, and the boys from the mines liked the entertainment. Tommy and me were friends. Now I know what you're thinking, and it started out that way for sure. But pretty soon we knew we had something better. He was a real thinker and had the smarts to buy up shares in those mines. He was going places and we both knew it. Heck, he loaned me the money to buy the Lead Pants. But after that it was strictly business between us."

"So, you and Tommy weren't seeing each other in 1917?" asked Saul.

"Nope. Ima came to see me night before last and made me tell her all about it. Seems she got her eyes on some papers that made it look like she and Schott here have the same grandfather. But it just isn't true. I had taken up with another fellow who run off right after he stole a week's worth of receipts. I never even put his name on Ashley's birth certificate. If he couldn't be bothered with the poor kid, I sure wasn't going to make anyone remember his name."

"And Ashley is Ima's father?" prompted Stella.

"You got it folks!" exclaimed the old woman gleefully. "They aren't cousins at all. Soon as they both know the good news, they can get hitched."

"Where is Ima?" asked Grayson.

"Well, I'm beginning to get a little bit worried about that," admitted the old lady. "She was supposed to meet me downstairs at four o'clock, and we were going to break the good news to Schott together. But she hasn't showed up."

"Where was she headed when she left you?" Grayson barked.

"She said she had to go tell her new boyfriend, Robert, that he was just a fling... a little over-reaction after thinking that she couldn't have Schott."

"And you haven't seen her since?"

"No, like I said, I thought she'd be here, but I waited half an hour and then came up to meet Schott for myself."

"Chief!" Stella exclaimed, "This must be the Robert she told us she met."

"Berry!" chimed in Saul Frake, "What's his last name?"

"Akesall. Do you know where he lives, Miss Basquette?" Grayson asked.

"Oh, yes, he's on Willow Place; 4321, I think."

"Berry," began Lt. Bragg, "that's two blocks over from Applewood."

"Bragg, we're going places," Grayson bellowed.

"Now, Berry, don't go off half cocked..."

"Bragg, don't you see, this may be life or death. Get in your car. Put on the siren and burn up the streets to that house. He's had her for thirty-six hours already. There's no telling what he's done."

"You can't ride with me Grayson. There are too many of you."

"Get going, Lieutenant! You can have all the credit. Just save that young woman!"

Bragg ran from the room, rousing the guard from his chair, and hustling the perplexed rookie down the hallway with him.

13

Stella Deet put her hand on Grayson's arm and gazed into his eyes with alarm. "Gosh, Chief, I hope there's still time."

"Let's go find out. We don't have a siren, but we can beat a few stop lights, I think."

Soon the three were zooming through the city with Frake holding tightly to the back of the front seat. "Take it easy, Berry," he begged.

"Saul, you just never do get used to this life, do you?" Grayson chuckled as he smoothly shifted down and shot through a boulevard intersection ahead of a lettuce truck.

They turned the corner at Willow just in time to see a man in a rumpled suit, with two days growth of stubble, being led from the house in handcuffs. Lt. Bragg held his arm tightly, and marched him to one of the squad cars.

"Come on," insisted Stella, "we have to find out how bad it is." She wrenched open the car door and ran toward the house. The police guard did not stop her. Inside, Ima Case was sitting on the floor rubbing her ankles. Lengths of cut clothesline lay around her on the rug. Stella rushed to the young woman and gave her a hug. "Miss Case, Ima, you're all right?"

Ima Case laughed ruefully, and said in a shaky voice, "Yes, I believe so. I just need something to eat and a few days to sort this all out. I think that nice Lt. Bragg has saved my life." She added, "I've made some very foolish decisions lately."

Grayson and Frake entered the room, and Stella announced primly, "Miss Case is considering being less cautious as concerns a certain young man." Stella squeezed Ima's hand. "Let's see if the police will let me fix you a cup of tea."

14

"When did you know, Berry?" asked Frake.

"As soon as you gave that name to me," he replied.

"Well, tell the rest of us, you sneak!" insisted Stella.

The three friends and Lt. Bragg were seated in Grayson's office. "Yes, Berry," the lieutenant drawled. "We found the barrel of the shotgun that Akesall sawed off in his garage. He had forgotten to get rid of it. The man had seriously begun to lose his mind. But how did you know?"

"The name Saul whispered in my ear was 'Mary Basquette Akesall.'"

"Who?" demanded Stella and Bragg, together.

"It took me a few minutes to figure it out," said Grayson, "but when we were listening to Violet tell her story I realized that if Schott and Ima weren't cousins, then Ima and Robert had to be. Violet mentioned that she was popular with the miners, and I guessed that there might have been other children besides Ashley. When I realized that, I knew that we had to act quickly because Robert was finding himself in a tight place. I called Violet last night and she confirmed that she and Tommy did have a daughter named Mary, but the girl ran away when she was very young, and the pain was so great that Violet never liked to talk about it. Mary was Robert's mother. Violet never knew that he existed, so when Ima told her grandmother about a Robert Akesall it meant nothing to her."

Bragg continued with what he knew of the tale, "Robert Akesall is seriously deranged. He must have killed Gunnildr before he sawed off the shotgun. The distance from the shell to the body makes that clear. Then he thought that he could make it look like the crimes were committed by different people if he changed the gun. But he overestimated the distance at which the shortened weapon would be lethal, so he only wounded Schott."

Grayson went on, "He apparently didn't know that Ima's grandfather wasn't Tommy Gunn. He thought that she was one of the heirs. Originally he decided that he could reduce the number of people who would inherit so that he and Ima would each get a larger share. He planned to marry Ima before she found out that he was her cousin. Then when they were married he could control both shares."

"When she went to meet him last night and told him that she wasn't an heir, he lost it completely."

"After that news hit him, he couldn't figure out how that would play out, Berry," added Bragg. "We had to put him in solitary confinement. He keeps muttering to himself, trying to make sense of it. He couldn't decide whether it was better to keep her alive because she wasn't an heir and therefore there was no reason to kill her, or if he should kill her because she was his cousin and she knew too much."

"In the end, it was probably that indecision that saved her life," concluded Stella.

14

The next morning Schott Gunn and Ima Case were seated at the hospital window, poring over a new copy of *Modern Bride*. Schott seemed as delighted as the smiling young woman. Neither seemed much the worse for their ordeals.

***

Berry Grayson inserted the latchkey into the door of his private office, but before he could turn the knob the door was pulled open from inside by a smiling Stella Deet. Saul was slouched across his favorite chair.

"Hello, Berry," he greeted his friend. "I brought the champagne."

"At nine in the morning, Saul?"

"Ask her," he responded, pointing his head in Stella's direction.

Stella dipped her head, and lifted her eyes to Grayson. "I've been thinking about the upcoming Schott Gunn wedding that isn't a shotgun wedding at all."

"Go on, young lady..."

"Young lady, my foot! We've been running around for three decades solving crimes and defending the innocent and we've never aged a bit. Crime scene techniques have changed, laws have become better; you even work with the police sometimes.

"But look at us... we are still young and bold and dashing and beautiful. One of these days we are suddenly going to find ourselves opening a book with you tottering over to that hat rack and my arthritic fingers stumbling across the typewriter.

Grayson grinned. "I think I get the idea, Stella. We'll still be efficient, but our popularity ratings will be shot. Readers want young heroes; they are naturally going to be attracted to someone who is a winner, who has smooth skin, and confidence behind the wheel of a big sedan."

"Right, Chief... I think our odds are running out. I have a proposition for you."

"Yes?"

"I'm ready to step out and experience the modern lifestyle. We can stop saying "gee" and "heck." We can see what year it really is outside of these pages. I think I see the last leaf of another paperback getting ready to slam down on our story that never changes."

"She's right, Berry. I need a vacation. You've worked me to death. I'm a nervous wreck from being dragged through your close shaves with the law, and riding in cars with you. I've lunched on greasy hamburgers and cold coffee till I have permanent indigestion. Truth be told, I'm tired of you always figuring out every case and not telling the rest of us until it's all done with."

"You might have something there," mused Grayson. "The case of the cautious couple didn't even make it to the courthouse. Milton Hamburger never got a chance to blow a gasket. I must be getting soft."

Stella raised her eyes to meet Grayson's. "I'm willing to get engaged, Berry. Maybe we could make that last another thirty years before we have to do anything drastic."

Berry Grayson gathered Stella Deet in his arms and pressed a kiss against her lips. Frake raised his glass of champagne and savored the bubbles despite the early hour. "To the most cautious couple!" he toasted.

"What the heck, Chief, let's get out from between these cardboard covers and have a life" Stella offered, when she came up for air. She ran to the edge of the page and prepared to leap into space.

Berry Grayson strode confidently to her side and took her hand. The breeze from the beyond the edge whipped her skirts. She laughed up into the handsome lawyer's face and jumped.

Grayson gathered his strong muscles and followed with a mighty leap. "I'm right behind you Stella," he yelled. "I've got the ring. It's been in my pocket for twenty years."

Counting on a Windy Lunch Hour

1 gull, pressed tightly against the wind

2 ships at anchor, oblivious

3 drops of spray spatter my thoughts

4 leaves, determined, headed northeast

5 doves lifting; slip-slide to a greener lawn

6 cares tattered in gusts of rearrangement

7 snatches of breeze-blown conversations

8 pebbles chatter; reprimand the waves

9 worries shattered, swept roughly away

10 sighs fragmented, scoured and scattered

freeing my spirits on this windy day

Expedient

MICRO FICTION – This story was written in response to a flash fiction prompt on Grandmas Goulash Blog. She regularly posted pictures as inspiration. The photograph is gone, but I believe the prompt showed a fly on a partially opened screen door. It would be great if there was a shadowy human holding a flyswatter in the background, but I no longer remember. Writers got extra credit for using the bonus word which was, that month, "expedient." The story had to be no longer than 150 words.

Ralph basked in the late afternoon sun. His future was an open door! It would be so expedient to enter–the odor of slightly spoiled warm bologna wafted past. He allowed his mind to drift–to become one with the enticing aroma in which he was now bathed. Eugene and Tyrone had long since flown through that portal into the heavenly realm beyond. Ralph hesitated for only one reason; his scouts had not returned. It was so unlike them to selfishly sate their own appetites without returning with bits of the treat stuck to their feet to present to him, the Fly King.

What could be the cause of their delay? Ralph knew that it was not prudent to follow without the report from Eugene and Tyrone, but, overwhelmed by the temptation, he raised his wings and buzzed into the kitchen.

Albums

Looking through old photo albums:
places, faces,
college chums.

Color pictures, black and whites,
good times, hard times,
travel sights.

Funny captions, stranger poses,
holidays and
special roses.

Hearts are kept in photo albums.
Softly, slowly,
love's glow comes.

17. The Bigg Building

The following is a chapter from *The Bigg Boss*, book four of the Dubois Files children's mystery series.

The children huddled around Mr. Dubois as they stepped into the Bigg Building elevator. "Fifth floor," he said.

"Step to the back of the car," ordered a tiny old man in a red jacket.

Only Cora had been there before. The scents of old, stained carpet and greased cables combined to produce an odor she never forgot. Cora rubbed her nose and adjusted the white blouse beneath her jumper where it had ridden up into her armpits.

The man reached forward and pushed down on a jointed bar that closed and locked the outer door. Then he stepped back and slid a brass gate across the front of the car. The gate showed a diamond pattern when it was closed. There was a brass shape like an upside down soup bowl fastened to the wall. It had a handle sticking out of the top. The man slid the handle to the left along the edge of the circle.

They heard a thump and a distant motor began to whine, rising in pitch. The floor jerked.

As oldest, Jimmie wanted to act sophisticated, and he tried hard not to reach out and grab the brass rail that encircled the small square room. *This paneling is real wood. Maybe walnut*, he thought. *I wonder if Mr. Bigg will listen to us. We're just farm kids.*

George and Ruby had never even been to Cold Rapids. Ruby stood with her mouth open, gazing at the ceiling. She whispered, "George, how can that light work when we're moving?"

"Electricity. See there are lights over there too." her brother pointed beyond the old operator to a panel with glowing buttons marked with words like "stop," and "call". "I don't know how they fasten the wires to a room that moves."

"The wires connect to the top of the car. They have to be as long as the elevator shaft is tall," Cora's father explained.

Laszlo had been in elevators in New York City, when his family had first come from Hungary. Memories of those visits to stuffy offices, and the slowing and bumpy adjustment when the elevator came to a stop made his stomach lurch. He hoped Mr. Bigg wouldn't be as unfriendly as some of the men his family had met with.

The diamonds of brass mesh scissored and disappeared when the operator opened the gate. As he released the outer door and slid it back, he announced, "Five."

They stepped soundlessly into an empty hallway covered in dark green carpet. Ruby tugged on Mr. Dubois' coat sleeve. "I have to pee," she said.

"Let's all be sure we are calm and prepared," said Mr. Dubois, as he led them toward the rest rooms.

Wanderlust

This poem was originally published in *North Country Cache*,
a collection of stories about my hikes on the North Country Trail.
North Country Cache received third place in 2005 for Regional Non-
Fiction from Independent Publishers.

Wanderlust
  has sprinkled
    Wonder Dust
into my eyes and ears and brain.

Wonder Dust
  has tickled.
    Go I must,
into the wind and sun and rain.

Wind's fey speep
  has prickled
    urges deep;
this restive spirit never tamed.

Sun shaft bright
  has flickered.
    Dappled lights
excise the crushing, brindled pain.

Rain soft cries
  have trickled,
    gath'ring sighs
to cascade, trembling, cleansing gain.

Wonder Dust
  has quickened
    Wanderlust.
Impatient voices call my name.

Midland to Mackinac Trail

ESSAY – This two-part essay appeared in the "Get Off the Couch" column in the *Ludington Daily News*, in September and October 2018. The column focuses on quiet outdoor recreation. Columns may be humorous, thoughtful, or informative. This entry was awarded third place in the state of Michigan from the Michigan Outdoor Writers Association, receiving the 2018 James H. Hall Award, for the best column featuring a non-consumptive activity (not hunting or fishing).

Part 1

The American Association of Retired Persons says that the reason time seems to pass so quickly as we get older is that we are no longer creating new memories. When everything is familiar and comfortable, time appears to flow past with increasing speed. I would like you to know that I've managed to slow time to a near dead-stop in the past week.

There's a hiking trail that not many people seem to know about, called the Midland to Mackinac Trail. It approximates a former Native American route from north of the city of Midland to the Straits of Mackinac. In 1957, Joe Brevirt, his Explorer Scout troop, and wife Willi, got the idea to try to resurrect a way to walk that former pathway. It was never one particular trail, and no written documentation exists, but with the help of Michigan's DNR and the Huron National Forest, a current route was established.

Boy Scout troops are assigned miles to maintain. With few people to care for so much trail, I'd heard that it was difficult to follow, and could be challenging, but I wanted to give it a try. Thinking myself to be a fairly experienced hiker, I upgraded some gear, dehydrated food like a maniac and thought I was ready to backpack those 210 miles in about 17 days.

Day one: I hiked 14 miles, and although I was pretty tired, I made my first day's goal. What you need to know is that a lot of those miles were on road. Friends of mine who live near the trail, and work on it, warned me to skip an entire section because of extensive beaver flooding.

Day two: lost the trail right out of my campsite. No blazes. Followed a farm lane to a road and walked around another few miles of trail. Got back on the trail. Notes on my map say "horrible." It was what I call bushwhacking with blazes, pressing from one blue mark on a tree to the next through chest-high blueberry bushes and ferns with no treadway. Wading through a series of 20 pond-size puddles in a two-track because the brush on each side was impenetrable. Camped well short of my intended goal.

Day three: Spent a total of 45 minutes looking for blazes throughout the day whenever I totally lost the trail. The blazes led me into a beaver flooding that was thigh-deep in water. Spent about an hour trying to get through that, eventually discovering there was wide and deep open water I could not pass. Called my friends to come get me, and hiked back to a place where they could access the trail with a car. Made it just past where I had planned to camp on night two.

Oh, have you noticed that the mosquitoes are brutal this month?

At this point I reassessed my plan. My friends began spotting me for day hikes, so I didn't have to carry the heavy pack. I have continued to lose the trail every single day, seldom making even my revised mileage goals. Bushwhacking quite a bit.

But I'm having an adventure. Making so many new memories that the past week feels about a year long. Listening to the barred owls in the dusk and the coyotes singing at night. A cool and beautiful rest at Secord Lake with blue water, a breeze and no mosquitoes. Fringed gentian. Always finding my way out of each predicament. Taking lessons in being humble. Trying to add memories of each tree and bush whenever I lose the blazes, so that I don't get really lost.

All I've actually lost is a little skin, one toenail, and about four pounds. I'm probably no less convinced of my ability to do this in some format.

Even if you are old enough to be receiving the AARP publication, you sure don't have to stop making new memories. I'm now on plan D, but still walking. I don't think I have time to finish the Midland to Mackinac Trail in this one trip, but I'll share the rest of my adventure next month.

Part 2

I did it. Finished the entire 210-mile Midland to Mackinac Trail, and it only took me 300 miles of walking to do it.

The temperatures backed down from unseasonably hot to a reasonable range for autumn which stifled the mosquitoes. That was a great relief, but then the rain began. It used to be considered a standard joke that if you went hiking with me—for a week or a only a day—you would get wet. In recent years, though, I'd managed to shed that curse and had delivered up beautiful weather for several long hikes with friends.

That vagary of fortune came crashing, well, dribbling and running, down around my ears nearly every day after that. I wimped out and started staying at inexpensive motels instead of camping. That turned out to be a perfect solution, since by then

Beaver pond along the M2M Trail

I had decided to write a guidebook for the trail, and I had a warm, dry place with electricity to work on it in the evenings.

Some days I cajoled friends into spotting me for a day's walk. One even stayed and hiked with me for three days. On twelve of the days, I walked out and back from my car, which meant I walked twice as far as the miles that counted. By one means or another, I hiked the trail, even if it took me a month to complete it.

As a Michigan long-distance hiking route, the Midland to Mackinac Trail is right up there with the best options. The North Country Trail has almost 1200 Michigan miles. The proposed

Iron Belle route will add mostly new bicycling options, as it plans to use the NCT for its western fork. The cross-state portion of the Shore-to-Shore horse trail network comes in at 220 miles, but the footing for walkers can be difficult. The M2M is 210 miles. One can devise a loop of around 100 miles on Isle Royale. After that, the mileages drop with the High Country Pathway at 80 and the Waterloo-Pinkney Trail at 36 miles. Of course, one can hike the many long paved multi-use trails, but these are usually less appealing to walkers.

I especially enjoyed the remote wilderness feel of most of the M2M. Despite the fact that hundreds of two-tracks, snowmobile trails, and old woods roads cut through the forests, the overall sense one has is that of serious backcountry. Tall spruce, aspen and white pine dominate some sections, while thousands of acres of jackpine are maintained by the state to protect Kirtland Warbler habitat. Most of the M2M lies across state forest land (Tittabawassee River, AuSable, and the Mackinaw State Forests), with some miles in the Huron National Forest. Small lakes with little or no evidence of human activity are common. The Michigan Elk Herd resides here, and although I didn't see an elk, I saw hoofprints. Also those of bobcat. The northernmost 34 miles are on rail-trail, and a number of miles are concurrent with less used parts of the Shore-to-Shore horse trail network.

Quite a few of the problems I encountered have already been fixed. With very few hikers taking advantage of this trail, maintainers become discouraged or apathetic about getting out there to keep up the blazing. Problems may not even be reported. This creates a downward spiral of interest, because not too many people are enthusiastic about struggling on a trail they can't find. If you are looking for a trail option that feels remote without driving eight hours, I suggest you get the trail guide and try out some sections of the Midland to Mackinac Trail.

In 2010, I stood at a small post in Mackinaw City (now replaced by a nice trailhead) which marked the junction of this trail and the North Country Trail. My interest was piqued and now that itch has been scratched. Thanks for coming along.

Trail guide can be purchased at Smashwords.com.

Friendship is a Frightening Thing

Friendship is a frightening thing.

To feel yourself letting go,

letting go of that tight knot
you've fastened round yourself,

letting the rope out inch by nich,
always aftaid to let go completely,

ready at any moment to snatch it back
and lace the cords tighter than ever.

A real friend can take up the slack
in your rope, and pull you close

gently, without jerking
or straining the threads.

At last you discover,
not unpleasantly,

that the cord encircles you both,
and is secured with knots of love.

The Room with No Name

MEMOIR – written as if it were the year 1976.

She was the second of my grandmothers to lie dying in the room, that room without a name. The other rooms in our house were sensibly called The Kitchen, The Dining Room, The Back Bedroom, The Back-Bedroom Closet, and so on. The closet in the un-named room, the only closet that was smaller than eight by twelve feet, even bore the ostentatious label: The Spare Closet. That small space was a mysterious realm having high shelves stuffed with closed unlabeled boxes, and seldom-shown pictures in frames. Enclosed stiffly in wood and glass posed Great-Great-Grandmother Cook from whose grim mouth it could be assumed no pleasant word had ever escaped. Brutus, the decades-dead St. Bernard wearing a studded collar, sat placidly among a tableau of prim ancestors. I was thirteen years old before I learned that the actual collar was also in that closet.

No one ever thought it was odd that the room had no name. It was always referred to by the things which resided there: "I left the notebook by the telephone," Mother might say, or "It's in the bookcase your father built." The room itself still seems featureless to me. The kitchen wallpaper was covered with small polka dots in primary colors, which on close examination turned out to be cherries, lemons or blueberries. The living room paper had white swirls on ecru, like some huge damask cloth. I don't remember the room with no name ever being painted or papered in all the years of my childhood.

But that day, that year, the room was defined by the hot, fetid presence of the old woman in the extra bed. At two minutes to three in the afternoon I entered the house slowly, as slowly as was possible after nearly running the two miles from school. I was expected to be home before my father left for work at three o'clock, to relieve him of the distasteful duty of caring for the woman in the bed, my mother's mother. Theirs was the least suitable match of caregiver and patient possible in my family. They radiated even more repugnance than I. They'd had decades of practice and I was a mere novice.

"Come sit beside me and hold my hand," was the inevitable, tremulous command. Postponing the odorous hours facing me, I headed first for the bathroom and then the kitchen to open a Coke. Finally, having no other credible excuses, I reluctantly sat on the edge of a chair near the bed. "If you loved me, you would hold my hand, my precious-one-and-only," crooned the skeletal woman.

Knowing that I would be reprimanded later by my mother if I did not comply, I allowed one hand to be clutched in the hot, dry claw. My skin crawled and my lip curled. In teenage churlishness, I did not even care if the woman saw. The odor of stale urine and oatmeal filled the room. *Why do old people always smell like this?* I wondered, as I wondered every day. My mind escaped to the cool grass of the hockey field, imagining the sharp crack of wooden sticks against hard balls. I resented the lost season with every breath of stuffy, acrid air.

"Read to me. Read 'The Wreck of the Hesperus.'" There were never any questions, only demands. It was just as well. No crumb of personal feelings would be shared with the remains of person in the bed. Reading at least provided an escape from any need for conversation.

> "At daybreak, on the bleak sea-beach,
> A fisherman stood aghast,
> To see the form of a maiden fair,
> Lashed close to a drifting mast."

The old woman seemed asleep, and I laid the book aside. With a jerk, and a tightening of the grasping fingers, her voice cracked, "Finish it! You know that's not the end." I fumbled to open the book again with my one free hand and read on to the dismal conclusion,

"Christ save us all from a death like this,
On the reef of Norman's Woe!"

"A drink, I need a drink of water." Seizing the moment of reprieve, I pulled my smothered hand free and held the bent straw to my grandmother's lips.

"Your father killed your rabbit, you know." The room reeled. There had been only one rabbit. It had disappeared when I was eight. They told me I had failed to close the door of the hutch, but I always knew better. "He was drunk." Now her lip curled, and an eye, suddenly bright, shot me a glance, sharp as an arrow. "He said that rabbits were meant to be eaten, not kept as pets."

I loathed this smelly lump of flesh that bore no resemblance to the grandmother I had adored as a toddler. The arrow found its mark. The father I thought I knew died, but I was buried beneath the soil of the woman's words.

***

Somehow time passes, in the room with no name, and elsewhere too. Graduation, college, a return to the hockey field.

Now, I am told my father lies in the room with no name, his face and neck covered with cancer lesions. I cannot recall the color of the walls.

Valentine at the Beach

The sun was cool, my soda warm,
I wandered, shiv'ring 'cross the sand.
The crabs, they scuttled o'er my toes;
O swell, my heart, the day is grand!

A horsefly bit; I cut my toe;
I heard a roar; the waves they crashed;
The wind, it blew me 'gainst the rocks;
I never knew my sandwich smashed.

'Twas such a day, like none before;
The gulls, they looked like turtledoves.
I never saw the great white shark;
It's all so clear; I was in love.

Autumn Cannonball

MICRO FICTION – This story was entered in a contest where the narrative was to contain exactly 53 words.

Bubbles streaming down. No, I'm blasting downward as bubble trails weave their upward dotted braids. The green becomes blacker; the cold becomes deeper. My toes tickle soft brown ooze. I flex my knees and blink. Suddenly shimmering above, a golden halo rippling, festooned with spiral hair. My head breaks through, entering October heaven.

Helen, who annoyed her Siblings and learned a Nature Lesson

CAUTIONARY TALE – This type of poem definitely requires an explanation. The form was perhaps perfected by Hilaire Belloc, in his 1907 book *Cautionary Tales for Children*. A sample title, "Jim, who ran away from his Nurse, and was eaten by a Lion," is typical. Modern readers unfamiliar with the genre may be appalled. The first public reading of this poem was at a open mic night where I read it without introduction. Needless to say, it was a popular as a slug at the bottom of a hiker's water bottle. Generally, a Cautionary Tale includes a stated taboo or prohibition: some act, location, or thing is said to be dangerous. Then, the narrative itself is told: someone disregarded the warning and performed the forbidden act. Finally, the violator comes to an unpleasant fate, which is frequently related in large and grisly detail. Consider it black humor with a moral.

Helen Mary Louise Prue, known as Helen Mary Lou,
So teased her baby brother Stu
That Stuart howled and Mother cried,
But Helen Mary Louise lied, and

Stamped her foot and rolled her eyes, "I did not
    pinch that baby's
Bum, " she wailed, and ran to Davy,
Her big brother. But she could not
Succeed in hiding all the rot inside.

Davy laughed, so making no effort to resist her
    muse,
she sprinkled pepper in his shoes.
Next morning Davy sneezed so hard
He fell into a tub of lard, but

HML, that naughty child, also had a sister Sue.
At lunch while dishing up burgoo,
Helen added Sue's pet goldfish
Simply to fulfill a wish. Their

Father, wise in nature's ways, warned Miss Helen
    Mary Lou
To heed the praying mantis, who
When young, would like as not,
Eat its siblings on the spot, with

Not a care, nor glance about. No parental chiding
    heard,
The mother mantis never stirred,
Nor clucked her tongue, nor uttered, "Stop!"
In truth, she'd just devoured Papa.

Next day, Helen Mary Lou stole the baby's candy
    cane,
Put Davy's toys out in the rain,
Read Sue's diary end to end.
And jumped until she broke the bed. Well,

Father, perhaps a trifle unobservant, never said
A word to her, this renegade,
And Mother, tired from washing plates
And spoons, and reading water rates, could

Scarcely find the time to speak to any of her
    children.
Stuart, tied to his playpen,
Davy's sheets with honey spread,
And Sue's best apron cut to shreds, bore

Mute testimony to the nature of our lively lass,
Not destined to be loved in class.
Sure, Helen Mary Louise Prue
Repented not, nor ever rued her

Playful pranks. So Sue and Davy, baby Stuart,
    marched into the
Pantry. Mother's handiwork was seen—
On the drainboard, by the pan,
Now sparkled bright clean forks and knives.

***

Neighbors noticed, stopped to say, "Quiet house, the
    children play
Politely." Wreathed in smiles, Sue and Davy
Overheard, not once but twice,
"And little Stuart's growing nicely."

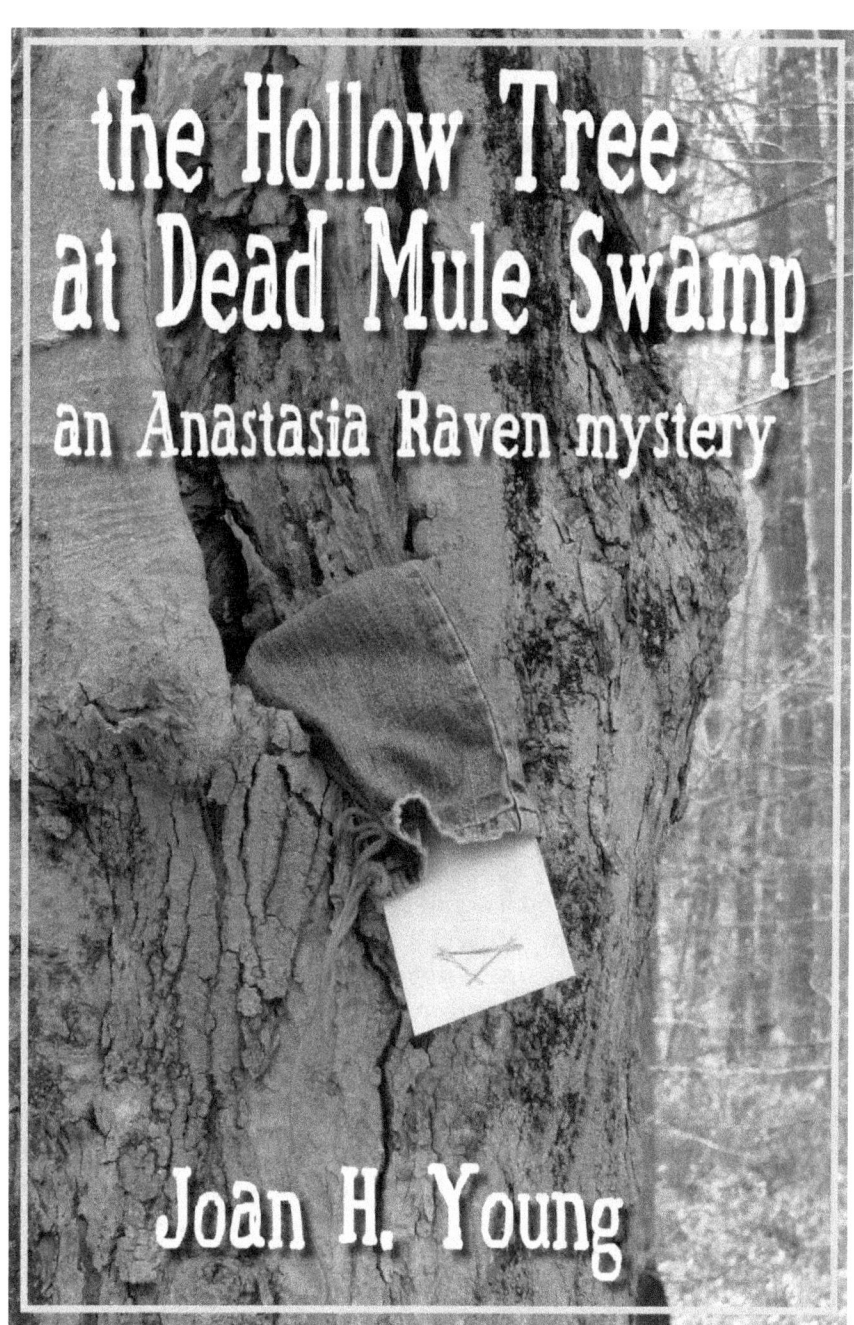

the Hollow Tree at Dead Mule Swamp

an Anastasia Raven mystery

Joan H. Young

The Hollow Tree at Dead Mule Swamp

MYSTERY – This is the second story in the Anastasia Raven mystery series, where Jimmie Mosher is introduced to the list of regular characters.

Black and white stripes filled the field of my binoculars and I momentarily thought a zebra had invaded Dead Mule Swamp. However, a quick adjustment to the rocker bar revealed the shape of a lovely black-and-white warbler, closer to me than was expected. I watched, fascinated, as it walked first up, and then headfirst down, the trunk of a large tree, searching the crevices of the bark for insects. Without ever spotting me, the bird fluttered off.

I was seated, somewhat uncomfortably, on a stump surrounded by poles stacked like a three-sided log cabin. It was a broken-down deer blind, abandoned by some hunter. I had come to Dead Mule Swamp about two months ago, but had only discovered the old blind two days ago. It amazed me that I, Anastasia Joy Raven, had changed in six months from a suburban housewife to a new divorcee who owned a fixer-upper house at the end of a dirt road in the Northwoods.

My former husband, Roger, had exchanged me for a partner named Brian, but I had left with a large settlement, paid in monthly sums, which should last the rest of my life, if I were careful. Our only son, Chad, was studying Wildlife Ecology at Michigan Tech. That freed me to try out the single lifestyle, and I was enjoying it. I was working hard on the house, presently finishing the living room, although that activity had been interrupted when an old newspaper found inside the wall had contained information which led to the murder of a neighbor. Frankly, I was glad that excitement was over.

I leaned down and lifted the bird book out of my daypack. Turning to page 243, and pulling my pencil from above my ear, I placed a check mark beside the warbler and noted the date, May 17. I returned the pencil to its resting place. My light brown hair falls around my face in a thick pageboy, and helps keep the pencil in place. Warblers are a bit of a mystery, but I was determined to learn a few new ones this year. The leaves were almost fully unfurled, and there wouldn't be many more days of easy birding.

It was early morning and the birds were moving about, so I raised the binoculars again and began searching the branches for unseen singers. As I scanned the trees, I caught sight of a piece of twine hanging from a large hole about ten feet up a tree. I thought the tree looked hollow, and wondered if a squirrel had pulled the twine up the tree for nesting material. However, when I followed the twine to the lower end I saw that it was looped around a small broken branch. It wasn't exactly knotted, but it didn't look like the kind of tangle that might have happened naturally. I went over to investigate.

I pulled on the string, and it rode easily enough over the scarred edge of the hole in the hollow tree. There was something with weight on the end, and I pulled until a blue cloth bag popped over the edge and dropped at my feet.

The bag was crudely made from the cut-off lower leg of a pair of jeans. Someone had sewed the bottom edge together with yarn, in uneven overcast stitches. The top had been gathered with the same yarn by using large stitches, making a drawstring, and the twine was tied to that. Obviously, whatever was in the bag belonged to some human. I was only a short distance off my own property, just beyond the west fence line. After my recent unpleasant experiences with a person chasing me into the swamp, I thought I'd find out who was using this tree for a safe or a post office.

I opened the bag, and there was a large white envelope and a small rock inside. On the envelope was a crudely drawn picture of three crossed twigs. I shook my head. Previously-it seemed a lifetime ago-I had taught literature at a community college. Although Nancy Drew was not exactly literature, my love for books extended to all genres, and I was sure I recalled a Nancy

Drew story where envelopes bearing a drawing like this were placed in a hollow tree, and then someone else would retrieve the message. I racked my brain for threads of the story. Those envelopes held cash which gullible women placed there thinking they were supporting orphans at the Three Branch ... something.

Well, I'd gone this far. I looked around and saw no one. The envelope was not sealed, so I probably didn't have to worry about being found out if I was careful to replace everything the way I found it. I slipped my thumb under the flap. Inside were two twenty-dollar bills, two fives, and seven ones. Behind them was a folded and wrinkled sheet of lined notebook paper. I replaced the cash, and opened the paper. On it, I saw the following:

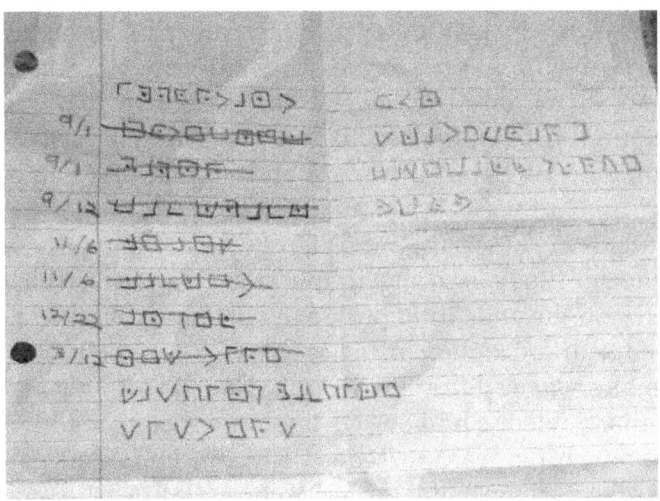

Obviously this was the work of a child. However, $57.00 was quite a lot of money to hide away in the woods. It seemed to suggest something more than a game. The code was a simple one, known to anyone whose children had played with cryptography at all. Even so, I couldn't translate it without making a key. I pulled a tablet from my backpack, and using the pencil again, copied the figures exactly. Then I replaced everything in the denim bag. It took me a few tries to throw the bag through the hole, but I quickly learned that the rock made this task easier, giving the bag some weight. I hadn't unwound the tangle that held the twine to a twig, so I was hopeful the owner of the stash would not notice the intrusion on his or her privacy.

This tree was only about a quarter-mile from my house, just off one of the many old two-tracks that led into the swamp. I followed it back to East South River Road, and then turned southeast, reaching my house in just a few minutes.

I set up a pot of coffee, and while it brewed, I tore a page from the tablet and wrote out the key that would crack the coded message:

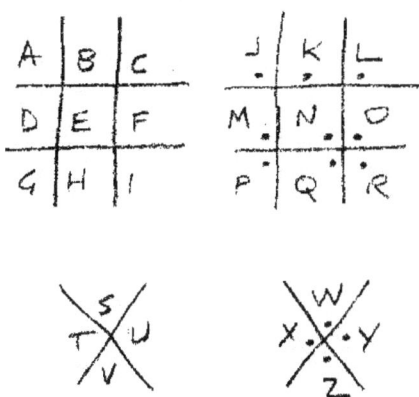

With my large midnight blue mug, the one with cream and brown glaze dripping down the sides, filled with fresh coffee, I sat down to translate the page. When I was finished I had the following two lists: Important, Fun. In the Important list the following words were crossed out with dates beside them: notebook, paper, backpack, jeans, jacket, angel, new tire. Below that, not crossed out, were: washing machine, sisters.

The list headed Fun contained three items, none of which were struck through: skateboard, baseball glove, X-Box.

My first reaction was that this must be a very determined young person to be saving money for such a long list, and secondly I thought it sad that he hadn't bought anything from the fun list. Except for the angel, it seemed like a list a boy would make. I finished my coffee and headed for the living room. My plans were to spend the day attaching board-and-bead wainscoting around the walls, which I'd painted a light

Wedgwood blue, with one end wall a slightly deeper shade. The wainscoting was going to be white. I'm handy with tools, and except for big projects, I was trying to do as much of the work on my house as I could without help.

As the day wore on, thoughts of the boy with the bank in the hollow tree kept crowding into my mind. The dates beside the entries led me to believe he'd been keeping money here since last fall when he'd bought school supplies and clothes. I wondered why he'd bought a tire—for the family car? The angel had me completely stumped, as did "sisters."

I thought school was still in session, and I called a friend, Adele, to confirm it. Adele owns a store in Cherry Hill, the seat of Forest County. Her family business is Volger's Grocery. She's a kindhearted and generous widow, but she loves to know everyone's business. I didn't want to tell her what I had found, but I knew she would have the information I needed. I punched in the number of the store.

"Volger's Grocery. How may I help you?"

"Hi Adele, this is Ana Raven."

"Ana! What are you up to?"

"Working on my house. Say, do you know what date school lets out? It must be soon."

"The last day is the 20th, the end of this week. Why?"

I had to think fast. "Oh, I might want to hire a boy to help me haul some trash out of the woods," I temporized.

"You remember Bella Hanford?" Adele asked.

"Sure," I said. I had gotten to know Bella just a couple of weeks previously. "But she's too small for what I have in mind." I didn't really have anything in mind, but there was that old manure spreader I wasn't sure how to get rid of...

"Not her. Her older brother, Thad, does odd jobs sometimes. Do you want me to talk to him?"

"No, no! I'm... um... just working on a list. I can call when I'm ready. But thanks for the tip."

"No trouble. Would you like to come to church on Sunday? The coffee and singing are good, and the sermon usually is too."

"I haven't been to church in years, Adele!"

"No better time to start."

"I'll think about it."

"OK, take care."

A little before three, I cleaned up the mess in the living room, took a plastic garbage bag and my binoculars and walked back to the old deer blind. The bag was to sit on. I knew I'd need to stay low to the ground to be hidden well enough from a human. By three-thirty, I was in place. By four-thirty, I was stiff as a board. No one had come to the tree. I was just thinking about taking a chance on standing up to stretch when an old bicycle with only one gear rolled down the mostly forgotten lane. I lifted the binoculars to my eyes so I could see more details. The bike had two plastic milk crates fastened to it, one on the handlebars, and the other on a rack over the back wheel. In the front crate I could see a number of shiny tin cans.

Peddling the bike was a thin boy with fair skin and black straight hair that fell into his dark eyes. He looked to be about ten years old. He glanced around, but didn't see me; then he pulled the bag from the tree. It looked like he put some money into the envelope, but I didn't see him add any marks to the paper. He quickly flung the bag back through the hole and pedaled off. My suspicions were confirmed, but I had no idea what to do about it. It wasn't any of my business, but I thought if I'd found the money that easily, someone else might, too. And, someone else might be perfectly willing to steal what was now more than $57.00. This boy was clearly worried about having the money taken by someone. Why else would he hide it so far away from where he lived? There were no houses within several miles of mine.

Giving the boy plenty of time to get away, I waited another twenty minutes before rising stiffly and returning home. I wanted to sleep on this puzzle.

The next morning, Wednesday, I awoke with the conviction that I should try to talk to the boy and decided I'd wait in the woods near South River Road. If I could find a good enough place of concealment, I would see when he rode down the old lane, and then stop him when he came out again. I left the house at two-thirty to give myself plenty of time to find a hiding place. I finally settled on crouching behind some honeysuckle bushes that were already fairly dense with leaves. It wasn't great, but it was the best I could do. This day, I brought a book, which made the wait more tolerable. I hunkered down behind the bushes till five o'clock, but no one at all, not a bicycle, a car, or a stray cat, came down the road. That was the normal amount of traffic on my back road.

I repeated my plan on Thursday, but this time, it worked. I watched the boy bike down the lane at four-thirty-nine—even with a book to read this was boring enough that I was counting the minutes. As soon as he was out of sight, I stepped out on the dirt road to wait for him. I managed to partially hide myself behind a tree. After a bit he came pedaling back, struggling slowly over the uneven ground, and I stepped out directly in front of him and grabbed the crate fastened to the front of the handlebars. I had to step back hard to stop the bike, but he had been moving so slowly it wasn't really difficult.

"Hey, lady!" he yelled, planting his feet on the ground. "What the f... heck do you think you're doing?"

"I want to know who you are." I said. "I just bought the house down the road."

"I know that. Everybody knows that. Are you going to try to keep people out of the woods?" He put his head down and worked the handlebars from side to side in an effort to shake off my grip.

"No, I can't do that. This isn't my property," I said. "I'll let you go, if you promise not to ride away. I just want to talk to you."

"All right," he said, but he didn't look happy. I released my grip, and he didn't ride off, but he did continue to glare.

"What's your name?" I began, but all I got in response was silence. "OK, how old are you?"

"Thirteen."

I lowered my eyebrows and pulled my lips tight.

"Well, twelve," he said, glancing sideways at something that might have been in the trees. But he did not try to pedal away. He was very small for twelve.

"Won't you tell me your name?" I continued more gently. "I'm Ana Raven. Not Anna, Ana, it rhymes with Mama." A film of tears suddenly sparkled in the boy's eyes. Something there had struck a nerve. "Do you have a mom?" I asked gently.

The boy nodded in the affirmative.

"Please tell me who you are. I'm not going to hurt you at all. If we are neighbors we should get acquainted. I didn't mean to frighten you, but I thought you'd ride away if I only called to you."

"I'm Jimmie Mosher," he admitted, as if it were the name of a criminal.

"Jimmie Mosher!" I couldn't keep the surprise from my voice. That's the name of a boy who used to live in my house. "

"That was my grandfather. I'm named for him." For a moment a bit of pride shone in his eyes in contradiction to the hangdog look of a moment ago, but then one of the tears spilled out and ran down his cheek. Jimmie ducked his head again to hide the supposed weakness from me and wiped his cheek against the shoulder of his t-shirt.

"Where do you live?"

"Over on Alder."

I racked my brain to remember houses on Alder. It was only a mile away, another dirt road, but I couldn't picture any homes there at all. "Do you want to come to my place for some milk and cookies?" I asked. I thought I had some cheap sandwich cookies in the cupboard. My enthusiasm for shopping is low.

"Uh, no. I gotta go," Jimmie said.

"Jimmie, I have to tell you something."

He looked at me warily and fidgeted. "What?"

"I found your secret."

"Oh, hell! Now I gotta move it. It's hard to find good trees."

"You're pretty young for that kind of language," I said sternly. I was glad he ducked his head so he didn't see me trying to hide a smile. "I won't bother it, but don't you think it would be too easy for anyone to find? I'm sure there are hunters here in the fall."

"Now too," Jimmie said. "Turkeys. But no one found it before you."

"How did you get that much money?"

"I didn't do nothin' wrong!" His head came up and his dark eyes blazed in the pale face.

"I don't think you did. You seem very resourceful to me." I

glanced at the basket of cans, and saw there were also chunks of other metal besides aluminum.

"I pick up metal and sell it to the scrap yard," Jimmie admitted.

"That seems like a hard way to earn very much money," I said.

He shrugged. "I'm too young to get a real job."

"I have some things you could do to help me. I even have some old metal trash behind my house that needs to be hauled away. What if you did the hard work and we put the scrap in my Jeep to carry it, but then you could keep the money? I'll pay you something for the time, too."

"You'd let me do that?"

"Sure. You'd be helping me. Seriously, there's a lot of junk back there."

"I know. I've explored all around. I already took the small stuff. I've been inside, too. It was easy to sneak in. I liked to sit upstairs and think about my grandfather. But now you own it."

"School gets out on Friday, right?"

"Last day. Tomorrow."

"Come over Saturday, and we'll start. Unless you have another commitment," I added.

"I'm not busy at all," he said with all the gravity of a businessman making a corporate deal. "I'll come."

Jimmie didn't exactly smile at me, but he was no longer glaring defiantly. I figured the deal was sealed with the promise of more cash. He pedaled away to the west. Alder Road was a left turn a mile away.

Drawing on all my new-found resources in the Dead Mule Swamp area, the next decision was an easy one. I needed to see Cora Baker, the local historian. Not only was she the person who had told me Jimmie Mosher used to live in my house, but she had hinted that she had dated him when they were young.

I called her that night and asked if she could tell me more about the previous owner of my home. She suggested I visit her the following day. We pooled our resources to come up with a lunch.

So, late Friday morning, I drove to the southwest corner of

Forest County, to a small house on the banks of the Pottawatomi River. In a cooler I had egg salad sandwiches on whole wheat bread and a jug of lemonade.

Alder Road was not out of the way at all, although it certainly wasn't the fastest route to reach Cora's. I turned south on the little-used road, and drove slowly, looking for dwellings that might be set back within the trees. I really couldn't remember seeing any houses along here. However, after crossing the defunct railroad tracks, and going around a jog, in about two miles I saw a house. At least, it might loosely be described as a house. An old semi-trailer had been parked in a small clearing, and a rough set of steps led to a door cut in one side. On the back was tacked a lean-to structure made of warped plywood, broken cupboard doors, pallets, and other scraps. A blue tarp was draped over this shed. The yard was filled with broken plastic chairs, old tires, buckets, damaged and rusting vehicles, and punctured bags of small trash with fluttering contents spilling through the holes.

"Oh, my Lord," I said out loud. "Can this be where that boy lives?" Alder continued for another mile before running into Fox Road, and that was the only possible dwelling place I saw anywhere along the way. "And he has a mother and sisters. What can I do that won't injure his pride?" I wasn't in the habit of praying, but this was the closest I'd come in a long time.

At Cora's I carried in the cooler, and she brought out a jar of homemade pickles, and plates. She'd already placed a container of brownies on the table. We sat at her kitchen table and ate lunch immediately. I liked Cora's old-fashioned kitchen that hadn't been done over since the 1950s. The one anomaly was a nearly new glass-top stove. Cora was no-nonsense, and when an appliance died she replaced it with one of quality. However, the most remarkable thing about Cora was that she had a genuine museum in her large pole barn. I had learned she wanted it to be in town where people could visit, but all I knew about the situation was that the topic was very upsetting to her.

After lunch, we went out to the museum. She'd been working there all morning, and the building lights were already on. "I have some things to show you," she said.

I was learning that there was nothing Cora liked better than answering questions about local history. When she could back up her answers with evidence, she beamed like a little girl, instead of a woman in her sixties. Cora was slight and usually wore overalls with a pastel shirt beneath them. This day was no exception, and the shirt was a lime-green gingham check. Her gray braids hung loose, although sometimes she pinned them up.

"Look at these pictures," she instructed, leading me to a work table near the middle of the large room, which was ringed with professional exhibits. "I rummaged around and found some gems!"

On the table were several old photographs with thick backing. I picked up the largest one.

"That's your house not long after it was built," she said.

The sepia picture was definitely my house, but the full-grown maples I loved near the end of the driveway were mere sticks. A team of dark horses was hitched to a large wagon. On the wagon sat a woman wearing a white blouse and heavy skirts, and a suited man with whiskers and a bowler hat on his head. I turned the picture over and read the spidery writing aloud, "Jedediah and Maybella Mosher, 1896." There were also individual pictures of the same man and woman.

"Those are the grandparents of Jimmie Mosher."

I almost did a double take, but then I remembered I hadn't yet told Cora about the young Jimmie, and she was referring to the grandparents of his grandfather. Cora rarely left her house. Local history was very real to her, but I wasn't sure she knew much about the current generation.

Next she led me to the corner of the museum with the replica of Judge Reuben Pierce Oldfield's bedroom. "See the fancy lights?"

"Of course." The curved, gilt brackets beside the bed ended in beautiful, etched glass bell globes.

"Those actually came from the Mosher house. When the place was re-wired I got Jimmie's parents to give these old fixtures to me. Most houses had pretty much the same kind, so they fit here perfectly."

"Do they still work?"

"No, just decorative." She sighed. "I don't have a good picture of the house when Jimmie lived there, but these are from my personal photos." She handed me a small album bound with leather, into which she'd placed a bookmark.

I turned to the marked page. These snapshots were of a type I recognized from my own parents' albums. I didn't think of Cora as old enough to be my mother, but she was. And there, in a number of black and white photos, she and a thin young man with dark hair were smiling at the camera. He looked very much like the boy I had met the day before. As I turned the pages, I saw them playing croquet, picnicking on a beach, and paddling a canoe. The last page contained posed pictures from a high school graduation. Everyone had taken turns standing with each group of people until there were pictures of almost every possible grouping. In the background was a red brick building. I recognized it as the now-empty, former Cherry Hill School. I pointed at the adults in the pictures. "Who are these people?"

"Those are my parents, and here are Jimmie's. Their names were Jedediah, Jr (everyone called him Jed), and Hazel. The Moshers, that is."

It was difficult to find an appropriate way to ask the questions that filled my mind.

"You want to know what happened. Why I married John Baker, and not Jimmie Mosher, right?"

"It crossed my mind." I grinned sheepishly.

"I was a stubborn little fool. Remember I told you how I'd been collecting historical things since I was a child?"

I remembered. Just a few weeks ago, Cora had shared with me her lifelong love for history which had resulted in this private museum.

"Jimmie wanted me to give it all up. He was a lot of fun, but he thought my collections were silly."

"You couldn't work out a compromise?"

"One day he wanted to teach me a lesson about what was important. He took a pile of my papers outside and set fire to them."

"Oh, no!"

"It turned out they were nothing important. He'd staged the trick with my mother's help. But instead of learning anything, I sent him packing. That was the end of our relationship."

"What became of him?" My interest was now intense, because a son of this Jimmie would be the father of mine.

"He went downstate and met a girl who went to the same college. Her name was..." Cora wrinkled her nose and pursed her lips "...Sandra Sue. Much more modern than someone named Cora with dust on her nose. Anyway, he got a degree in business and moved back here with Sandra Sue. They opened a restaurant. It's the empty building just west of town on the highway."

"Where are they now? Did they move away?"

"Both dead. Killed in a car wreck." She sighed heavily.

"Did they have any children?" Of course I knew they must have had a boy.

"One son, Lee, who also had a son, I believe."

"Don't they live around here? Why didn't he keep the family homestead?"

"It's one of those local tragedies. The son and grandson were in the car too. Only the baby survived. His mother moved away. I don't know what happened to the baby after that."

We had opened a couple of folding chairs while we were talking, and now we sat there in silence for a few minutes while I thought over what I should do. Cora must have realized I had something on my mind because she waited patiently. "Are we through with these?" she finally asked.

"For now," I said.

Cora bustled around putting the photos back into cases stacked along the long wall near the newspaper archive.

When she was finished she came back and sat down again.

"I have something to tell you," I began.

"I thought perhaps you had," she said, rubbing a small hand over her lips to hide a smile. "Did you find another great secret in your house?"

"No, this secret is much more lively."

"Oh?"

"Cora, I've met the grandson. His name is Jimmie Mosher, too."

Her eyes opened wide. "Where is he? How is his mother? I don't remember her name."

"One thing at a time! I don't have very many answers. He apparently lives in a complete dump on Alder Road. I think his mother is alive, but he almost cried when I brought it up." I didn't want to mention the sisters, because I wasn't yet ready to betray Jimmie's secret list.

"We have to do something to help him! Can we go over there now?"

This was a remarkable request, because I knew Cora only went out when she felt there was an event she couldn't avoid. "Not so fast," I insisted. "I just learned all this yesterday. The boy doesn't trust anyone, but I think I might win him over. Give me some time, OK?"

Cora agreed, but she was clearly agitated. We spent the rest of the afternoon puttering around the museum. I really liked Cora and admired her local history projects. The upshot was, I volunteered to come out once a week to help her sort boxed items and enter them in the database in her very new computer.

I told her I planned to see the boy the next day, and she sent the rest of the brownies home with me.

Jimmie, the grandson, pedaled into my yard just before nine Saturday morning. I could not believe how thin the boy was, but now that I'd seen his house, I suspected his girth was not only genetic, but perhaps because the only meal he ate each day was the school lunch. But now school was out for the summer.

I brought out gloves for the both of us, which he complained about, but finally put on his small hands. I knew he picked up old metal all the time, but I decided I didn't want him getting tetanus at my house, or his house, whichever it was.

The rusting manure spreader I'd been trying to get rid of was going to require a tractor to pull out from where it had taken root in the yard, but behind that was a brown pile of broken iron wheels, buckets, gears, and many unidentifiable objects. Jimmie hadn't lied. Anything small enough to fit in his milk crates had been removed. I backed the Jeep across the lawn so we didn't have to carry things very far, and folded down the back seat. Some of the items required us to work together to pull them free of the mess. By eleven, we had filled the back of the Jeep.

"You're all right, Ana," Jimmie finally said. He'd hardly spoken all morning.

"Thank you," I replied, gratified that I'd measured up to his exacting standards. "How much money do you think you'll get from this?"

"Steel is $75.00 a ton." The boy certainly spoke like a midget businessman.

I strained to do some math in my head. "But that's less than half a cent per pound!"

"Yeah, but it all adds up. Aluminum is worth a lot more. And people throw out a lot of cans. Copper's even better, but if you take in very much they think you stole it."

"How much money can you make?"

"Most days I manage a couple of dollars. I'll have more time to hunt for stuff now that school is out. Let's get going. The scrap yard closes at noon on Saturdays."

We climbed in the Jeep and traveled mostly in silence. Jimmie directed me with minimal words to Harold's Scrap Yard, about four miles away, on the north edge of Cherry Hill. When we arrived, a woman in a booth waved us onto a scale, and I drove cautiously over the platform. In a minute she waved us on and we continued to the back of a large metal building. Mountains of metal scrap, more kinds than I'd ever thought about, were scattered around, with narrow driveways between the piles. Jimmie pointed to one of the mounds. We drove there, where a friendly man with no teeth helped us unload. "This is Gus," Jimmie said. "He's my friend."

"Hello, Gus," I said.

The man wiped a rusty palm on his greasy pants and extended it. I shook hands, trying to remember that dirt wasn't necessarily the same thing as germs. "Hi, Missy," he said, nodding and bowing.

"OK, bye, Gus. See you next week," Jimmie said to the man. "Now we go weigh the Jeep empty," I turned the vehicle around, and on the way back to the scale he added, "Gus isn't very bright, but he likes me."

"Don't you have friends?" I asked.

"Wait. We have to get paid," a deft avoidance of answering me. The woman recorded our weight without the metal and Jimmie said, "I have to go in the office and get the money."

He came back in a few minutes, grinning from ear to ear. "We got sixteen dollars and thirty-two cents. I don't have to put the change in the envelope," he added.

"Who says?"

"It's my rule. The bag would get too heavy if I put coins in it."

"Jimmie, would you come and eat lunch with me?" I asked. "I have a tub of brownies, and I can't eat them all by myself."

"Really?"

"Really." I nodded at him seriously; another business decision.

After two peanut butter sandwiches, milk and a brownie, I tried to pry more information out of Jimmie.

"Tell me about your mom," I asked.

"She's nice," Jimmie answered. That wasn't much help.

"Is your family just your mom and you?"

"Nope."

"Who else lives with you?"

"Bert. He's my mom's boyfriend." Jimmie licked chocolate from his fingers, and looked longingly at the tub.

"Go ahead," I offered. "Eat all you want. What is Bert like?

"He's not very nice. I try to stay away from him."

"What does he do that's not nice?" I wasn't sure I wanted to hear the answer.

"He drinks too much, and then he likes to hit people. I just run away, but my mom puts up with it. I don't understand why."

I wondered if any answer I gave would make sense to a serious boy. "Sometimes women feel as if it's better to stay with someone and be abused than to be all alone."

"But she would have me!" Jimmie said. He sort of choked on a piece of brownie. "I don't want to talk about it any more."

"Fair enough," I said. "But, will you trust me a little bit?"

"Maybe. For what?"

"Why don't you let me keep the money at my house? I'm really afraid someone might steal it from your tree. There are a lot of bad people in the world."

"That's the truth," Jimmie agreed quietly. But he didn't say anything about me keeping the money.

I tried something else. "Why did you draw three branches on the envelope? I have to tell you they look just like something described in a book."

"I know. I read the book."

"You read a Nancy Drew book?"

"Why not? Are you going to tease me because they're for girls?" his eyes roved around the room as if he were looking for a place to hide.

"No, not at all! People should read whatever books they like."

"I finished all the Hardy Boys the library had. Nancy Drew is smart, and she fixes things for people without a lot of help."

"She does indeed! So you just liked the crossed twig design, or is there more? In the book it stood for something."

"Two things. First the bad guys called it Three Branch Ranch, and that was a phony investment scheme. But then they changed it to Three Branch Home, to get people to give money to help kids. But it was a scam."

"Why do you use it?" I had a guess as to part of the answer.

"Because I want to help some kids," Jimmie answered evasively.

"Your sisters?"

"How do you know about my sisters?"

"I don't really, but it was one of the words on your list."

"I'm going now." Jimmie said. His eyes were hard. He grabbed another brownie and ran out the kitchen door before I could stop him. I hadn't paid him yet for his time. I stood at the window over the sink and watched him pedal away. Everything about his body language said "furious."

I did go to the Crossroads Fellowship church on Sunday morning. I figured a few prayers for Jimmie couldn't hurt. Adele introduced me to the pastor, Theo Dornbaugh. I knew almost none of the music, but I liked how upbeat it sounded, and the sermon included the Scripture that it would be better for someone to have a millstone put around his neck and be thrown in the sea than to hurt a child. I certainly agreed with the message in that verse. We didn't have a sea nearby, but there were a lot of rivers in the county.

After the service I had another question for Adele. I caught her during the coffee hour. It wasn't hard to find her; she was in charge of the kitchen.

Joan H. Young

I grabbed a cup of coffee and called through the pass-through, "Adele!"

"Ana! Come around here and talk to me." The kitchen door was closed, but I pushed it open and entered. No one seemed to object. Adele had covered her ample frame with a flowered sandwich board apron and was rinsing spoons at the sink. "I'm so glad you came! Do you like our little group?"

"I hardly think I can answer that yet. But I would like to ask you something."

"Shoot." She shook off the spoons and placed them on a clean towel.

"Look, I'm really new here, but is there any fund, or some way, or..."

"Are you in trouble? I thought that man gave you plenty of money."

"It's not for me! Let me explain. I've met a little boy, and he has almost nothing. Even worse, I think his father beats him."

"That's pretty serious. Who is it?"

"He'd be really angry if he knew I was talking with anyone about him. He's very proud. I don't think I should say who it is just yet."

"Then we can't help much, can we?" Adele was put out. She wanted to know all the juicy details.

"Come on, Adele, be patient." I was put out too. "Give me a few days to win his trust. I just want to know if there is something that could be done."

"There's the Family Friends Committee."

"What do they do?"

"We try to find ways to help families in need. Sometimes we take them food or clothes, or we help them find jobs. Once in a while we can afford to provide a larger item or help with a utility bill. Things like that."

"That would really help this family, I think." I knew it wouldn't scratch the surface of what Jimmie really needed, but anything would be a start. "Do families have to apply?"

"Not formally, but they have to be willing to accept the help, and the committee has to agree." Adele accepted the empty serving plates from another lady and put them in the dishwater. She thrust a towel into my hands.

"Yes, I can understand that. I haven't even met the parents yet. Let me see what I can do."

"You should join the committee."

"Adele! I just came to church for the first time today." She handed me a wet plate, and I dried it.

"OK, come a few more times, and then join the committee."

"I'll think about it."

"That's what you said about coming to church, and here you are. I think you mean 'yes,' but just don't like to be pushed."

I took another plate from Adele and reflected that I understood how Jimmie felt when I asked him to do new things.

That afternoon, I had changed into jeans and was getting ready to work on my wainscoting some more when there was a soft knocking on the front door. I opened it and Jimmie stood there with his bag.

"Come in!" I said.

Jimmie entered and looked around at the sawhorses, raw wood sections, tools and general mess. His dark eyes gleamed. "You're doing this yourself?"

"I am. Most of it anyway. I'm not so good at drywall seams." I spoke to him as I would to an adult.

"I think my grandfather would have liked this."

"I hope so. I've seen a picture of this house when it was new. It was well cared for then."

"Really? Where's the picture?"

"A lady I know named Cora has it."

"Could I see it sometime?"

"We can arrange that." I said. I knew Cora would love to meet young Jimmie.

Abruptly, he changed topics. "I've been thinking about my bag. Maybe it would be good if it were here. But I don't want to bother you every day."

"It wouldn't be a bother."

He went on as if I hadn't said anything. "It would be OK if you kept most of the money inside. But I want to keep some of it in a place I know about, so I can get at it."

"That might work," I said. "Where is it?"

"I'll show you. Come on."

Jimmie led me outside, and around to the back of the house. There is a stone basement under the two-story portion of my house. It's not very useful because it's damp, but it has an outside entry with a slanting hatchway door. He opened one of the sides of the double door and started down the wide concrete stairs. I opened the other side to let in more light and followed him down. On the steps were several old crocks. Jimmie found one that wasn't broken, and he turned it upside down.

"I never wanted to use this place before, because people do poke around old houses looking for stuff. But now that you live here, it will be safer. I'll put my bag under this crock. Here in the shadows you can hardly see it anyway."

"I think it's a perfect place! Let's go back inside, and I'll pay you what I owe you, too"

"You owe me money?"

"Yes, I said I'd pay for your time on Saturday."

We walked in silence into the house. He put his envelope on the kitchen table, and I put a twenty-dollar bill beside it.

"How much change do you want?" he asked.

"None," I said. "That's yours."

"Geez, that's too much!" he said, looking at me in horror.

"Not at all. We worked for three hours. That's not even minimum wage."

"Nobody paid me money like that before. They think I can't work hard because I'm so small"

"You proved to me you work very hard," I said. "Take it."

Jimmie carefully laid his money on the table. He put the seven ones back in the envelope and handed me the remaining $89.00. He'd already put the $16.00 from yesterday in his stash, and he'd added money two other times when I'd watched.

"How much does a washing machine cost?" he asked.

"I'm not sure. I think you can get a basic one for about $400.00."

Jimmie's face fell. "That's an awful lot."

"It is. Maybe you could find a used one that still works well."

"That sounds better."

"Jimmie," I began. This was going to be difficult. "I drove past your house. Is that really where you live? In that old truck?"

He hung his head and nodded. Then he added, "I only live in the shed."

I was appalled, but tried to keep my voice even. "Why there?"

"Bert doesn't like me in the house, and Mom won't argue with him. She thinks he built me a nice place. It's not so bad. I fixed it up a little bit. I've got a mattress. And it doesn't leak with the tarp over it."

"That's good." I couldn't think of much to say. Instead I got up and pulled the peanut butter out of the cupboard, and set it in front of Jimmie with the bread and a knife. "Want jelly?"

"Sure!" Food was always a good way to cheer up a growing boy.

"What is Bert's last name?"

"Fowler," he said, eagerly spreading peanut butter thickly on a slice of bread.

"What's your mom's name?"

"Desiree, but she likes to be called Dee. My parents were Dee and Lee. It was like a family joke. My dad died in a car crash. I guess I was in the car too, but I don't remember." He spooned jelly on top of the peanut butter.

"How do you get enough money to live on?"

"Mom gets a check for me, because Dad died. And another one because she's sick. But Bert takes the money because Mom has to sign the checks for him to cash. She doesn't go out. She used to be ok, but now she weighs too much."

"And he drinks?"

Jimmie nodded again. His mouth was now full of sandwich.

"Jimmie, I don't want to make trouble for you, but would your mom talk to me? Maybe I could get her some help. Maybe we could get her a separate bank account that the checks could be sent to so Bert can't get the money."

The frightened look came over the boy's face again. "She'd lick me too, if she knew I'd told you about Bert. He says he'll kill her if she rats on him. I think he would."

"All right. We'll wait on that. But I'm going to think hard about a way to fix this. You do know that most boys don't live in sheds with a tarp for a roof, don't you?"

"Yes, but it doesn't make anything better to think about it," he said with glum wisdom.

I wrote Jimmie a receipt for the money I would keep for him, and he put the seven dollars in the bag under the crock on the hatchway steps. I gave him the peanut butter and jelly and the loaf of bread. He tried to refuse, but finally relented when we slipped it in a plastic bag and put it under some empty beer cans in one of the milk crates. I couldn't understand how a child could be too frightened to bring home food. And I still knew nothing about the mysterious sisters. I hadn't dared bring that subject up again.

Jimmie and I slipped into an easy routine for the next week. I decided I might get more answers from him by giving him a way to communicate without being embarrassed. Sunday night, I worked out a message in his tic-tac-toe code and slipped it into the envelope along with a pencil. I first asked him, "Why an angel?"

Late Monday, I saw Jimmie slip into the back yard. He hadn't ridden his bike up to the house, but had come in from between the trees. I didn't go out to talk to him. However, after he left I checked under the crock, and he'd answered, also in code, "Christmas for my mom." That made sense. I was extremely pleased that Jimmie seemed willing to answer personal questions via code.

He came to the hatchway each day, and by the end of the week I'd learned his sisters' names were Beth and Lindsey, that they were seven and four years old, and that they lived with their father, somewhere in Iowa. From this information, I deduced Dee had a boyfriend or husband between Lee and Bert, and the girls were Jimmie's half sisters.

Writing coded messages was not all I did that week. I spoke to both Adele and Cora about the situation, now that I knew the boyfriend's name was Bert Fowler. Adele immediately knew who he was, and told me with barely suppressed anger that the county had been trying to do something about that family for months. She said no one would file a complaint because of Fowler's violent temper and general threats to kill anyone who interfered with his family.

Since Adele know pretty much what everyone was doing most of the time, she also told me Bert hung out at the Dead Dog, a local bar, some week nights, but always on Saturdays. She also said Dee Mosher had once been a good-looking vibrant woman. When Lee was killed she had married again, and moved away. Adele didn't know where. But when Dee moved back to Cherry Hill, she was overweight and depressed. She'd spent too much time at bars and the truck stop in Emily City. Then she'd taken up with Bert and all but disappeared from view. That was three years ago. But Jimmie came to school, was clean and not a discipline problem. He never had any visible bruises. Everyone could see how they lived, but there wasn't an obvious reason to file a complaint. Sure, the boy was thin, but so was his grandfather. Most everyone remembered that Jimmie Mosher, and Lee, who'd owned the Cherry Blossom Restaurant.

I asked what Bert looked like, and she told me he was about fifty, not yet fat, but going bald on top, so he wore a cowboy hat. He had a waxed mustache and a swagger that made him stand out.

Cora was excited about meeting Jimmie, and she urged me to bring him to visit her. I promised her I'd try to work something out. It seemed as if no one kept track of the boy well enough to mind if he were missing for a few hours. He apparently spent all day riding the back roads looking for metal. And Jimmie had said he'd like to see the pictures. I just had to work out the logistics.

Meanwhile, it was Saturday, and I decided I wanted to meet Bert. I put on my tightest jeans and a scoop-neck t-shirt. When I added some flashy dangling earrings and eye makeup, the effect was terrible, but it seemed to fit with what I had in mind. A little after nine that evening, I walked into the Dead Dog and blinked. The interior of the bar was really dark. As my eyes adjusted I saw the usual line-up of men at the bar, and some couples at the few scattered tables. Loud country music was playing, and I recognized the tune of "If I Die Young." I could hear the clacking of pool balls, and a rumble of voices competing with the loud tunes.

I walked to the bar, and ordered a draft pale ale. I'm not much of a drinker, but I knew I could handle a couple of beers.

While the bartender filled a tall glass from the tap I looked down the bar. Sure enough, a few people away to my right, was the man who had to be Bert Fowler, mustache, cowboy hat and all. Most of the men were wearing baseball caps, and no one else had a handlebar mustache. I had to admit, he was handsome enough to be attractive, if I hadn't known his dirty secrets.

A few heads turned to look at me, but nobody paid too much attention. I didn't recognize anyone. I sipped my beer and started watching a baseball game, which was playing on the TV mounted high in the corner. The sound was turned down. I was struggling to read the tiny ticker at the bottom of the screen, to see if I could tell who was playing, when there was Bert at my right elbow. Maybe this was going to be really easy.

He leaned sideways into the bar. He had on a denim shirt with the sleeves turned up loosely to reveal hairy forearms. The shirt was tucked neatly into a pair of stone-washed jeans. His belt had a large Mack Truck buckle, and the jeans tapered to where they met tooled cowboy boots. His face was tanned and the mustache was perfectly rolled. "I don't think I've seen you in here before," he began.

"You haven't," I agreed.

"What's the occasion?"

"Oh, nothing special. I've lived here a couple of months, and just haven't had time to get out much yet."

"Can I buy you a drink?"

"I have one, thanks."

"That's pretty tame. How about something stronger?"

The man's not shy, I thought. I covered my glass and laughed. "Oh no, I'm strictly a beer drinker."

"What's your name?"

"Ana Raven. I bought the old Mosher place on East South River Road." I wondered if that would get a reaction.

"Hey, we're neighbors," he joked. "Name's Bert Fowler. I live out that way too." But he didn't flinch at hearing the Mosher name, and he didn't mention the dump on Alder Road.

"Do you have a family?" I asked.

"Not me," he boasted. "I'm a free spirit." The man just beyond Bert guffawed, but it might have been at the error the shortstop had just committed. I thought it would be perfect to be hearing the strains of "Your Cheatin' Heart," but I didn't recognize the tune that was playing. I sure recognized the music Bert had in mind.

"How about you?"

"Divorced," I admitted.

"A pretty lady like you?"

I took another sip and tried to look demure. I doubted I knew how, but it was worth a try. "Where do you work, Bert?" I asked.

"Here and there. Used to drive truck." I couldn't haven't made up a more useless answer. "Do you play pool?"

"Oh, not very well. But I'd like to watch you play." At least that would give me a chance to observe him, without talking too much more.

He nudged a man seated a couple of stools away. "C'mon Bud, let's rack 'em up, and show this honey how it's done."

Bud and Bert made their way to one of the pool tables, and slapped a stack of quarters on the rim to signal the players they wanted the table next.

I followed along bringing my beer. Soon it was our turn, and Bert pulled the balls from the side slots and arranged them in the rack. Stacking the quarters was only a custom, as the coin slot had been removed. Playing the game was free. Bud chalked the cues. I spent the next hour leaning against a dirty wall watching Bert show off some of his best swagger. It was almost nauseating to keep raising an eyebrow, smiling, winking, chuckling at stupid jokes, and praising the man for good shots, but I did learn that Bert was going out of town on Wednesday on some sort of delivery job.

He tried to convince me to stay longer, but I said I was tired, which was certainly no lie. I was plenty tired of Bert. It concerned me a little bit that I'd told him where I lived, but it wasn't like my address was any secret around town.

Now I understood more about why people were reluctant to make any complaints about Bert. He was handsome and personable, even if not my style. If Dee was grossly overweight and ill, people probably felt sorry for Bert. As long as there was no obvious evidence of abuse, no one was going to stick out his or her neck. Couple that with Adele's assertion about his temper, and it all made sense. It wasn't right, but it made sense.

Jimmie was unlikely to visit on Sunday, since Harold's Scrap Yard wasn't open that day. After church (which seemed cleansing after my evening in the bar with Bert), I called Cora and asked her if she'd like to meet Jimmie on Tuesday. She was emotional with anticipation but tried not to let me know how strongly she felt about Jimmie. To give her something more mundane to discuss, I suggested that we fix a nice lunch. Since Cora likes to cook and bake, this turned out to be a great idea. I tried to get her to let me bring some food, but she wouldn't hear of it. She did agree to let me do the shopping, since she doesn't drive. As a result, I ended up with a list of groceries to buy on Monday.

There was one thing left to do that day. I sat down with my code key and laboriously printed out a note for Jimmie, telling him I could take him to see some family pictures on Tuesday. I suggested he come in the house tomorrow and talk to me about it.

Monday was Memorial Day, and the small town of Cherry Hill was preparing to celebrate in a humble way. I didn't yet feel connected to the community enough to care to watch the small parade that was scheduled to take place in the early afternoon,

Luckily, Volger's Grocery was open in the morning, catering to people who had forgotten to buy their picnic supplies. There, I bought the ingredients for sloppy joes, plus potato chips, some vegetables to cut up, dip, and ice cream. It seemed like a simple menu, but a safe one to please a hungry boy.

"Put that ice cream back in the freezer for a minute," Adele said. "I want to talk to you."

I didn't mind the order, because I was confident Adele had enough influence with the right groups to actually get Jimmy and Dee some help. "What's up?"

"You left right after the service yesterday," she accused.

"I didn't have any reason to stay longer." I didn't understand what the problem was.

"This is a small town. When you are trying to get things done, you have to spend time talking with the people who can help you."

"Did I offend someone?" It sounded like I'd offended Adele, for sure.

"I wanted to introduce you to Glenn Erickson."

"Who's he?"

"He's the head of the local Habitat for Humanity group, that's who! He doesn't come to Crossroads all the time." She added as an aside, "His wife is Lutheran."

"Are you thinking we might get a house for Jimmie and his mom?"

"Exactly! But we'd have to get Dee to agree to leave that bloodsucker Bert. We're not building any houses for him! I don't know anyone who is friends with Dee, though."

"I haven't even met her."

"But you're so good at figuring out how to get things done," she wheedled.

"I'll think about it," I said.

"You are thinking about a lot of things, Ana. Better make up your mind."

I rolled my eyes, retrieved the ice cream and headed for Cora's house on Brown Trout Lane.

Cora was in a dither. Other times I'd spent with her, she'd always been calm and organized, but she was nervous and flitting from the cupboards to the table and back.

"Do you think we should use china plates? Maybe paper is better for a little boy?" she worried.

"Cora, I think you should calm down. If you're like this tomorrow, you'll scare the poor child away. He's very serious."

"Oh dear, his grandfather was such a clown. Maybe I'll do everything wrong."

"Jimmie hasn't had many chances to laugh. He acts like a little businessman." I chuckled. "A hungry businessman."

"That sounds like my Jimmie. Both parts!"

"Look, he doesn't know much about his family, but he used to sneak into my house to think about his grandfather. He knows about the accident, and that he was in the car."

"That poor boy." Cora shook her head.

"I think you should just do what you do best. Show him the

family history and he'll be delighted."

"Do you really think so?"

"I do. Just be yourself, and he'll like you."

She shook her head in wonder. "He could have been my grandson."

I gave her a little hug, and we worked together to make the sloppy joe filling, so it would only need to be heated tomorrow. When I left, she was mixing sugar cookies, convinced that ice cream was not enough dessert.

Late that afternoon, Jimmie slipped in from the trees again. I had been watching for him, uncertain whether he would come on a holiday, but hopeful that perhaps he'd earned some money running errands or something. Soon, I heard a gentle knocking on the door at the head of the basement steps. It had taken me a long time to translate the plan into code, but I thought it might appeal to Jimmie's sense of adventure and love of secrecy to come in through the cellar. I'd left the door at the bottom of the hatchway steps open, and suggested he come in that way, and up the inside basement stairs to the kitchen. That way no one would see him coming to see me. I opened the door at the top of the dark stairway.

Jimmie grinned. "That was fun," he said.

I smiled back, "I thought you might think so. How about some soup and a grilled cheese sandwich?"

"Sure!" he said. "But you feed me every time I come."

"I have a son, but he's at college now. I know boys are always ready for food."

The tomato soup was in a pan, and the sandwiches were made and ready to grill. I had been confident he'd be willing to eat. While I heated the soup, Jimmie pulled another twenty-dollar bill from his pocket and put it on the table.

"Here's more for you to keep. I've got over $100.00 now," he said.

"Great! I want to tell you about the lady we are going to see."

"OK."

"Her name is Cora Baker, but she will be happy to have you call her Cora. She knew your grandfather very well when she was young."

"Is she that old lady with all the old stuff in her barn? We were supposed to go there on a field trip from school, but the bus couldn't get down her road, so it was cancelled."

"Yes, that's the place. Look, Jimmie, Cora dated your grandfather for several years. They broke up before he went to college and met your grandmother, Sandra Sue. She cared for him a whole lot."

Jimmie thought about that for a minute, but didn't say anything.

"How does that make you feel?"

"I dunno. I think maybe I like it. I like to talk to my grandfather Jimmie, just pretend of course. He tells me what to do sometimes, when things don't make sense. She's really talked with him?"

"Lots and lots. Want to know a secret?"

"Yes!"

"They broke up over a stupid practical joke, and she's been sorry ever since. But you can't tell her I told you."

Jimmie grinned. "It's a deal! How do we get there?"

I told him where it was, but he was worried about Bert finding his bike anywhere near home. He insisted on riding at least part of the way there. He wouldn't even agree to put the bike in my cellar.

So, the next morning, I met Jimmie at ten at the corner of Centerline and School Section Road. He pushed his bike into the bushes where it was well-hidden, and rode the rest of the way with me in the Jeep.

Cora had composed herself overnight, and she and little Jimmie hit it off instantly. He was delighted to see the pictures of his great-great grandparents, but held the book with the photos of his grandfather with care approaching reverence. He asked Cora to tell him the story behind every single picture, but at the same time seemed to have an innate ability to stop just short of asking embarrassing questions. I was mostly a spectator, but I was happy to be there.

He ate three sloppy joes, much to Cora's delight, and an extra scoop of the ice cream, not to mention potato chips, cookies, and a handful of carrots.

By mid-afternoon, he was calling Cora "Nana," and was accepting little around-the-shoulder hugs from her. In short, the day was a huge success.

Before I dropped Jimmie at his bike, however, I had to warn him about a part of my plan that might not make him so happy. Since I'd learned Bert was to be out of town (if I could believe him), I had decided I'd try to talk to Jimmie's mother, Dee. When I told him I was going to visit her the next day, however, he didn't object at all. He did say he would stay out all day, that he didn't want to listen.

He agreed to help me with one thing, though, because I certainly didn't want to show up before Bert was gone. Jimmie said he'd wait till Bert left, and then ride past my house as a signal. But he insisted he couldn't stop, that I'd have to watch for him through a window.

After I saw Jimmie pedal by in the morning, I waited another half hour, and then drove over to the truck-house on Alder Road. I carefully pulled into the yard, and climbed the steps to the door. It was actually a standard exterior door, fitted into an opening cut and framed into the semi-trailer body. No use hesitating. I knocked firmly.

After several minutes the door was opened by a grossly overweight woman in a pink sweat suit. She was breathing heavily.

"We don't want to buy anything," she began.

I smiled my best I-care smile. "I'm not selling anything. I'm Anastasia Raven. I bought the old Mosher house. I've met your son, Jimmie."

"Oh," she said.

"May I come in? I'm sorry, I don't know your name."

"Dee, Mrs. Dee Pickard." She seemed uncomfortable, but finally said. "OK. I guess it's all right."

She stepped back and I entered the made-over trailer, expecting the worst. I was shocked beyond any expectations. Instead of being a mess, the interior was clean, well-lit and tastefully decorated. The only thing to complain about was a lack of windows. The space had been transformed to be very much like the inside of a standard trailer. There were too many knick-knacks for my taste, but it certainly wasn't my house. The primary theme was angels. I wondered which one Jimmie had given her for Christmas.

"Have a seat." She pointed to the couch and waddled to the easy chair facing the television. I was afraid I was going to have to compete with game shows, but she picked up the remote and clicked the tube off.

"Mrs. Pickard," I said. I was still so shocked I hardly knew what to say. "I'm concerned about Jimmie."

"But school's over for the year, isn't it? Did he lie to me and skip the last week of school?"

"No, nothing like that. Jimmie seems very responsible."

"What's he done, then?"

"Nothing bad. Honestly, Mrs. Pickard. Let me explain. Jimmie works very hard to earn enough money for things that are basic needs for a school child."

The woman didn't answer but she leaned forward, clasped her hands, extended her arms and pushed them between her knees. She began rocking forward and back.

I had to press my argument. It might be the only chance I'd have. "He has hinted to me that there might be problems with Bert."

She continued to rock.

"Is there something you'd like to tell me, Dee. May I call you Dee?"

She nodded.

I didn't have high hopes for real information on this visit. I knew abused women often refuse to admit they are in trouble.

"Is there a reason Jimmie had to buy his own winter coat?"

"Bert won't give me any money," she whispered.

"Not at all?" I asked, looking around.

She saw my eyes roving over the knick-knacks. "These things are mine from before. Bert leaves them alone if I'm good." I wondered what that meant.

"What about things Jimmie needs?" I insisted.

"Bert doesn't like Jimmie. He makes him stay out back in a cabin he built for him. Jimmie says it's nice." There was a desperate note in her voice. She wanted to believe it very much.

I closed my eyes for a minute, then said, "Have you seen his room?"

"I can't get out, really."

I thought I saw my opening. I asked gently, "Would you like to see where Jimmie lives?"

"Can you help me down the steps?"

"Of course."

It was not a simple project. The truth was, even though she had to be ten years younger than I am, Dee could hardly walk. But she sent me to a closet where I found a cane, placed on a high shelf, out of her reach. That seemed particularly cruel.

Getting to Jimmie's room took almost an hour. Dee could only take a few steps before she had to rest. I brought out a kitchen chair and she perched on it for several minutes after walking each five or six feet. She was so large, her behind rolled off the sides of the chair and she seemed to have trouble balancing on the seat. When we finally worked our way around to the back of the trailer, she looked around, confusion showing on her face.

"Where is his cabin?" she asked.

"Right here," I said, pointing at the low lean-to made of scraps of wood with the blue tarp battened over the top. I thought for a minute she was going to fall off the chair, but she took a deep breath, and struggled to her feet again. We continued the slow march. I wasn't sure I was going to be able to find the door, the shed was such a patchwork of different surfaces. But when we got close enough, I found one board with hinges on the edge, actually a cupboard door, and an old-fashioned latch obviously salvaged from Jimmie's scavenging. I pressed the thumb button and the bar lifted out of the hook. I pulled the door open and bent over to look in. The roof was only four feet high, not tall enough even for Jimmie to stand up.

"Sit down and wait a minute," I suggested to Dee. I crawled inside the cave-like space.

An electric drop cord was tacked across the ceiling and hung near the door. I reached out and pushed the button; the small room flooded with harsh light. The walls and ceiling were lined with odds and ends of pink and blue foam insulation board, cut and fitted together like a crazy quilt. The floor consisted of a couple of pieces of plywood laid directly on the dirt. A scrap of torn, stained carpet led from the door to the opposite wall. To my right, under the low end of the shed, I saw a bare mattress with a neatly arranged, but odd set of coverings, including a sleeping bag, a blanket, and a torn canvas tarp. Wooden potato crates were stacked along the walls for shelving.

I backed out of the doorway, and said, "You need to see this. Let me put the chair by the door."

Dee stood up and waited till I got the chair placed beside the opening so that she should be able to see in if she leaned forward. She got settled and began to examine Jimmie's "cabin." I couldn't see her face, as it was turned into the small door, and I wondered how she was reacting. However, her body language began to send me signals. I saw her heavy shoulders rise and fall once, then again. Her knuckles tightened on the handle of the cane, which she held with both arms extended as a prop.

After almost five minutes, she pushed on the cane and sat upright. She still didn't speak, but seemed to be fumbling with her clothes. I wondered if she'd been bitten by a spider or something. But in another few seconds I realized she was simply lifting her sweatshirt. She turned her face to me and said bitterly, "Look at this."

All around her ribs and across her stomach were bruises both new and old. Some were purple; others had faded to yellow and green. I raised my eyebrows.

"I'm not sure I can get in a car anymore, but I'll try if you can take me to the police station. Bert Fowler has told me one too many lies."

Just then, Jimmie appeared from behind some oil barrels that were stacked at the edge of the clearing. Obviously, he'd been hiding to see what might happen as a result of my visit. He ran to his mother and put his arms around her neck.

"Why didn't you tell me, son?" she asked, as the tears began to run down her cheeks.

"I didn't want to make you sad," he said, rubbing her on her back.

"Can you be strong, if we go to the police? Bert will be awful mad."

"Maybe he'll go to jail," Jimmie said hopefully.

"Not forever," Dee said, shaking her head. "But we better not worry about that yet."

Dee could not lift her leg high enough to step into the Jeep, but I managed to pull in beside the open steps that led to the trailer, and with our help, Dee awkwardly got into the passenger seat. Jimmie hopped in the back, and we headed for Cherry Hill.

"We need to go to the Sheriff's Department, I said. You live outside the Cherry Hill village limits."

"Oh, no! I can't do that," Dee said. "I want to talk with Tracy Jarvi."

Tracy is our young, female Chief of Police. She's very popular. In fact, Tracy is one of my favorite people in my new hometown. She was doing a terrific job of making friends and slowing down the rate of petty thefts and vandalism that can pull a small town into a steady decline.

"She'll just have to turn the case over to the county."

"Well, she can do that if she has to. But I saw her on television. I think she'll understand. I'm not talking with any Sheriff."

I hadn't met the actual Sheriff, and knew the case would probably be handled by a woman detective, but I didn't want to do anything that would make Dee change her mind, so I drove directly to the Cherry Hill police station, which is located beside the court house, just north of the village park. I pulled into the parking lot and stopped in the shade of a tree.

"I can't get out," Dee contended. "Maybe she can come out here?"

Jimmie reached over the seat to pat his mom on the shoulder reassuringly, and I went inside to explain things to Tracy, and ask her to come outside.

Tracy and I returned to the car in a few minutes. I was still afraid Dee might chicken out, but apparently she really had no idea that Bert hadn't even provided Jimmie a heated place to stay over the winter, and she was now thoroughly angry although frightened. She poured out the story to Tracy, who listened and asked appropriate questions. In addition to the bruises on her mid-section, Dee also showed us black-and-blue spots on her arms and legs.

Dee was winding down her story, and Tracy said she would go call the Sheriff's Department. She tried to assure the unhappy woman that no one was going to blame her for Jimmie's living conditions.

After Tracy left, Jimmie spoke up. "What about Beth and Lindsey, Mom?"

"I don't know, Jimmie-boy, I don't know. Their dad has custody, but I'm sure we can visit them if I can lose some weight. I don't know how I got this way."

"OK, I miss them."

"I know you do. I'm so sorry," Dee whispered.

"It's OK, Mom," Jimmie whispered back.

"Three branches?" I asked, and he nodded.

Tracy returned in a minute and said a deputy was on the way, and also an ambulance to take Dee to the hospital in Emily City. Emily City is actually in the next county, but Forest County's population is so sparse, we only have a small out-patient clinic.

"They'll want to do a forensic examination, and check your general health, Mrs. Pickard," Tracy said.

"Oh, is that necessary?" Dee looked uncomfortable.

"Absolutely. You want to make these abuse charges stick so that Bert Fowler can't get revenge. The case will be even stronger if he's been preventing you from getting necessary medical treatment."

"OK," she said in a small voice.

"From the things you've told me, he's already looking at domestic abuse, child endangerment, and theft. Lets make sure we do it right."

I looked at Tracy and nodded in full agreement.

Tracy continued. "It's going to take at least a half-hour for the ambulance to arrive. They said it was still out on an emergency."

Dee added quietly, "Bert said he'll be gone till tomorrow sometime, so I guess a few more minutes won't matter."

"How about if Ana and Jimmie walk over to the Pine Tree and get you three some lunch? We'll buy," Tracy said. This was the second time I'd known Tracy to buy a meal for a witness. It was an interesting police tactic, but I was sure Jimmie would be happy. For all I knew, Tracy was buying the food with her own money. "Just tell them to put it on my tab," she added.

Dee said she wanted a tuna sandwich and some kind of fruit, with a diet cola to drink. I was surprised she didn't order a hamburger and French fries, based on her size. I have to admit I don't always feel very compassionate toward heavy people.

Jimmie and I walked east on Lincoln to Balsam, and then south to Main and to the Pine Tree Diner. It was only a couple of blocks. The small restaurant is Cherry Hill's one surviving eatery. It won't win any awards for décor, but the food is always excellent. We were soon on our way back toward the police station with two bags filled with food and several cans of pop. We each carried one bag. I'd ordered the same as Dee, but Jimmie went for the burger and fries. However, he wasn't in any danger of getting fat soon.

Because it's a prettier walk, and because it's also slightly shorter, instead of taking the same way back, we cut through the village park. The park pretty much fills the block bounded by Main and Mill Streets to the south and west. The Petite Sauble River, the same river that creates Dead Mule Swamp near my house, runs on through town, and forms the north border of the park. To reach the park we only had to walk west on Main, about a half block. However, this took us past Volger's Grocery.

Adele's radar must have been working overtime. I have no idea how she knew we were there, but she was standing on the broad stone stoop, under her big maple tree, waiting for us as we passed the store.

"Hello, Ana. I see you've made a friend." she said.

"We only have a minute, Adele. Someone is waiting for us." I was trying to be circumspect. "This is Jimmie Mosher. Jimmie, Mrs. Volger."

"We know each other," Adele said. "Jimmie shops here." I suddenly realized he probably bought most of his food with the spare change he kept from the envelope.

"We have lunch for my mom," Jimmie said proudly.

"Oh? Where is your mother?" Adele was clearly fishing for news.

"She's at the police station. We're not going to live with Bert any more." I was surprised the secretive Jimmie would give out so much information, but Adele has that effect on people.

"Good for you!" Adele's ample bosom jiggled as she nodded her pleasure.

"We should be going," I said. "The food, you know."

"Sure, sure. Come see me later."

"I will," I assured her.

"Nice to see you," she added, to Jimmie.

"Things will be better now, I know they will," Jimmie said to her over his shoulder as we walked on. "She's nice to me too," he added to me. "I know she usually gives me more food than I pay for, but she doesn't like me to say anything about it."

We crossed the street and entered the park. A sidewalk followed the east side of the park, behind a row of stores, until it reached the river, and then angled northwest to follow the water until reaching Mill Street. Mill is aptly named, as a shingle mill was once located where the river passed beneath the bridge. The water along this section was channeled into a mill race, and although the mill is long gone, the concrete walls of the race still force the water into a speedway, where it moves quickly, even in summer. Now, in the spring, when the water was high, the liquid churned and boiled through the deep, narrow space. A fence separated pedestrians in the park from the dangerous channel.

At Mill Street we turned north and crossed the bridge. A truck door on the opposite side of the street opened, and Bert Fowler approached menacingly. He must have come home early and found Dee gone.

"What are you doing with my boy? You've got no right, you bi...."

"Run, Jimmie!" I hissed, spinning around and pushing him back in the direction we had come. I hoped Jimmie would run around the block and get Tracy or Kyle, the deputy. Or maybe Tracy and Kyle. At least the river prevented Bert from getting around me to reach the boy. I turned back to face the angry man.

Bert advanced. "Where's Dee?"

"Dee?" I asked, feigning ignorance.

"You lying witch. Don't you think I know she's in your car at the police station?" I'd heard the expression "mad with rage," but I don't think I'd ever realized it could be a real condition. It seemed as if his eyes were on fire.

He sprang toward me, and I struck with the only weapon I had, swinging the bag of food at his head. Fortunately, the cans of soda were in my bag, making it heavier than the one Jimmie had been carrying. The bag broke, and Bert's cowboy hat was knocked to the street. The action must have surprised him because he stepped back. A fruit cup had burst and bits of melon lodged in his hair. He wiped juice from the side of his face, and a can of 7-Up rolled away into the raging water.

I saw it go out of the corner of my eye, and I didn't like how vulnerable I felt on the bridge. The railing was as old as the bridge itself, made of rusting, fitted pipes and very open. Not all that high, either.

"Now you are going to learn not to mess with me," Bert growled. He unzipped his jacket and I saw the grip of a handgun protruding above his belt.

I stepped back, not daring to turn away from him, and he reached for my arm. Just then, a shot rang out, and Bert stumbled, clutching his left shoulder.

"Hold it right there, Bert Fowler." Tracy must have come from the police station, and down Mill Street. She was now standing on the opposite side of the street to get a good angle on us.

All in one motion, Bert reached inside his jacket and turned to face Tracy. She shot again. I didn't see where the bullet hit, but the force of the blow pushed Bert against the railing. His slippery cowboy boots scrabbled on the old concrete, and he grabbed for the railing, but his left arm, at least, was useless. Without a word, he went over backwards into the roiling flume. The last thing I saw were his eyes boring into mine, still filled with hatred.

You might think no one would have attended the funeral of a man like Bert Fowler, but you would be wrong. There was no church service, however, only a short graveside observance. Of course, his friends from the bar were there. I only knew Bud, and at that, I didn't know Bud's real name. But, Chief Tracy Jarvi went too, just because the police attend local funerals. I went to be with Jimmie, who insisted he wanted to see the man be put in the ground. The local press was represented by Jerry Caulfield, distinguished owner, editor and primary reporter for the *Cherry Hill Herald*. He stood next to me at the graveside and attempted to ask me questions for a human interest story, before the burial service began. Although Jerry was a nice person, I was uncomfortable answering with Jimmie at my other side. Of course Adele was there. She never missed an important Cherry Hill event.

Dee, however, was still in the hospital. As it turned out she was, indeed, not well. Her obesity was due, for the most part, to serious hypothyroidism, which had gone untreated for at least the three years she had been with Bert. They were trying to stabilize her, and to get her medication levels adjusted. Jimmie was overjoyed that his mom was going to get well.

The ceremony was brief, and to the point. No one, not even Bud, had any eulogies to give for Bert Fowler.

After the service, Jerry Caulfield and Adele walked with Jimmie and me back to our cars.

"You should thank Adele this service wasn't for you," Jerry opened. His tone was lighthearted, but I knew he was serious.

"So I've heard."

"She called the police just as soon as she saw Bert Fowler get out of his truck."

"That cowboy hat always did make him easy to identify, and there's a clear sight line from my store right through the park," Adele said."

"Thanks, Mrs. Volger," Jimmie added. "I was running around the block, but I couldn't get there any faster because of the river." He sounded apologetic. "And I dropped the lunch too."

"That's all right, Jimmie. You were doing just the right thing," I said. "You got away, and Tracy got there in time."

"Come by my house, Ana," Jerry implored. "You certainly don't want next week's *Herald* to print an incorrect version of events."

I still wasn't used to the concept that everyone had to know all the details of every local event. However, I had to admit a shooting on the second-busiest street in Cherry Hill was probably news. "I'll call you," I promised

Jerry accepted this, and headed off to his car.

Adele was simply bursting with something she wanted to share. "I have just the most wonderful thing to tell you. You and Jimmie both. Mostly Jimmie, actually." She turned to him, "But first, I want to be sure you have a place to stay."

"I'm staying with my new Nana for a few days," Jimmie said, grinning.

"Nana?" Adele looked confused. I wondered how this would go, since Adele and Cora don't get along very well.

"He's staying with Cora until Dee is out of the hospital," I explained. "She has two empty bedrooms."

"I could have stayed at our trailer. I can take care of myself," Jimmie put in.

"We know, but the county doesn't like that plan," I said.

"Aw phooey, I could do it," Jimmie added. However, he didn't sound upset about spending time with Cora.

"Oh, well, I guess I can understand that. His grandfather was crazy about her. That woman has no sense," Adele said in a huff.

"I want to learn all about my grandfather Jimmie Mosher, and maybe open my dad's Cherry Blossom Restaurant again. The Pine Tree is OK, but we need another place to eat here."

"I'm sure you can do it, if you put your mind to it," Adele said.

"Jimmie is a pretty good businessman already," I added. I put a hand on his shoulder and smiled at him. "But maybe you'll need to wait at least until you're out of middle school."

"Maybe," Jimmie admitted reluctantly.

"Well, here's my good news," Adele said.

"Yes?"

"I've been talking with Glenn Erickson."

"The Habitat for Humanity guy?" I asked.

"Exactly. He thinks this will be one of their most worthy projects ever. They are going to fix up that old house at 714 N. Dogwood Street for Dee and Jimmie. It's right on the edge of town."

"I know where it is!" Jimmie exclaimed. "I already cleaned up the empty cans there. It's got woods in back and a big yard.

We could have chickens and a pony."

"What would you do with a pony? You're going to be too big for one before long," Adele said.

"Beth and Lindsey will come, at least for the summers, and we will be the Three Branch Ranch."

"I hope so," I replied. "I hope so."

Adele had just one more topic on her mind. "Ana, you really will call Jerry Caulfield, won't you?"

"Oh, all right. I suppose it will be better than having someone make up a story about what happened."

"You know, he likes you."

"Adele, for heaven's sake!"

"Just promise me that if he asks you on a date, you'll go."

This was really too much to take, especially with Jimmie there. I said, "I'll think about it."

"Ana," Adele warned, "you are thinking about way too many things. It's time to do something."

Secret Spring

My father told me about the secret spring
    the year I turned fourteen.
I thought I had explored every inch of our small
    farm.
Yet we walked the lane to the farthest woods and
there he searched, revealed a hollow filled with
moist leaves and a faint burble of life.
He turned to me and smiled.

The Shark's Wisdom Tooth

My nickname is Sharkey. I've had it since I was twelve years old, and there are segments of the population who know me by no other name. It is often shortened to Shark. Here is some of the Shark's philosophy of living.

Nobody cares how smart you are.

You don't have to talk to be a good conversationalist. You just need to ask the other person questions. Develop a list of questions you can always fall back on.

Everyone has at least one good quality and one deep hurt.

Everyone has something to contribute.

Never take the interstate if you have time to take the back road.

If you've got it, use it- let others flaunt it.

"Never give up" may only be bull-headed, not right-headed. Be sure you can tell the difference.

Everyone has a handicap; some people's are just more obvious than others.

Everyone has some area of life where they are not following God's perfect plan for their life; some people's are just more obvious than others.

Spend money on experiences not things.

60, 30, 15, 10, or even 5 minutes spent on a project or towards a goal gets you closer than saying "I don't have time today."

Just because someone doesn't say "thank-you" doesn't mean they are not thankful.

Just because someone doesn't seem to change their mind doesn't mean that you have not influenced their thinking.

If the cause is important, then win, but you don't have to win just to have a good time.

Agawa Canyon Train Trip

Train speeding through autumn woods
Unfocus my eyes
Bargello-weaving red, green, gold, bronze leaf-wool

Indigestion

The train crawls,
a segmented silver worm
with rumbling indigestion.

Two Minutes of Water

LITERARY FICTION – This story has been entered in several contests, but the highest praise it ever received was from the man who founded Ludington Writers. George Dila proclaimed, "That's a good story!" If George liked your work, you knew it was pretty good.

I never saw anything. An unnatural breath of wind prickled my skin, a vague sensation that all the oxygen was being sucked out of the air, and the ground gave a little ripple under my feet. I didn't look back.

Luckily, I was only fifty yards from the entrance to the Catacombs, Unit III. The first three levels were office space, and the work day had just ended for most people, so the escalators were crowded. Seven of the eight stairways were lifting people to ground level, but I didn't care. I flung myself at a moving line of men and women and pushed my way through them, screaming "Down! Go down!" No one listened until they reached the surface and saw the mushroom cloud that was surely rising behind me.

"The blast doors will close in five seconds." The perfectly calm voice that came over the loudspeaker did nothing to quell the pandemonium that ensued as the escalators abruptly changed direction, carrying everyone back into the safety of the earth. "Please take refuge below Level 10. The blast doors will close in three seconds. Please take refuge..."

I had a head start on almost everyone, and I was fast, unhampered by the tight clothes and shoes of those who were dressed for work. I leapt over railings as I approached each floor and never stopped till I reached Level 12.

Once there, I had to face the reality that my own shelter pod was in Unit II. I had nowhere to stay.

Then I saw her; we had been friends in school. Her hair was

longer now, soft brown, flowing down her back. Her natural smile was straightened into a line of concentration. "I'm in the wrong unit," I said, looking down at my ratty sneakers.

"Come with me."

For the next few days we huddled with a thousand other people in the common rooms at the bottom of the Catacombs, Level 20, living on bottled water and chalky, pre-packaged meals. Lights, fans and pumps ran off generators powered by a token quantity of the force that had sent us scurrying to the depths. The steady voice from the intercom kept us updated, but it did more to annoy than to calm us. After three days of living like refugees, we were allowed to return as high as Level 5.

She led me to Level 6. Just beyond the escalator was a white-tiled communal bath where a row of semi-partitioned toilet bays ended at three uncurtained shower stalls, the walls angled for some privacy. Assuming we had forgotten the rules, the too-calm voice announced at regular intervals that a timed shower every other day was allowed. If one entered a shower stall, a scanner in the doorway read an implanted microchip, and the water began if a shower was due.

Her room was five doors past the bath. Each pod was like every other, except for size, and owners were required to stock essential provisions that would last two months, but some people chose to do more. She had. A small table was neatly laid with a red flowered cloth. A dry sink in the corner adjoined a small counter and drawer unit. There was a small microwave oven. The rest of the room was lined with shelves. These were filled with non-perishable foods, carboys of water in the lower racks and a few drawers with see-through fronts. I could identify the faded indigo ends of folded jeans, multi-colored sweatshirts and thick white towels. She had loaded a free-standing unit with books. I also noticed a double deck of cards and a Boggle game.

There was one narrow cot in a corner. "It's a single," she said. There was no apology in her voice, only explanation. The pod was a duplicate of mine in Unit II, except that hers looked nicer.

"It's OK. I'll get a pad from below," I said.

We settled into a routine of reading, playing games, and eating plain, but adequate, meals. We never talked about the future.

Four days later, the rumors began. "...blast door damaged when it closed." "...hammering on the secondary seals." Bored after losing another game of Canasta, I decided to sneak up to Level 1, which was now open to unlucky officials.

Before I reached the doors which led to the escalators, I knew the rumors were true. Great splintering blows could be heard from the other side. These inner doors were wooden, mostly decorative, with carved designs. Then, the unthinkable happened; the end of a crowbar poked through the heavy panel. I ran and leaned all of my puny weight against the door. A hand, horribly burned, clutched my arm. I came face to face with a head, it was hard to call it a face, there was no nose. Deep, discolored eye sockets were framed by straggling clumps of hair. Most of the hair had fallen from the scalp leaving raw, red sores. More arms reached in, touching me, fondling my clothes and my face.

As the last shreds of the door crashed inward, I turned and ran, sprinting down the stairs as I had before. I left my shirt on Level 3. Peeling my jeans was more difficult, but by Level 6 I was running naked toward the bath. I had forgotten about the automatic switch, and it was not my day, but one shower was in use.

I barged into the stall. She was there. We clung to each other and wept as two minutes of water swept over us.

Silent Tears

Behind a veil of silent tears
              I wait
for no one who has ears
              to hear.

July 22, 2010

I sat on the stoop
composing bad poetry
in my head. You're gone.

The Third Person

EPISTOLARY MYSTERY – This short story presented in the modified form of a variety of documents won first place in the Accentuate Writers contest on the theme of "vengeance" It would have appeared in the anthology, *Expressions of Passion*, to be published by Twin Trinity Media, however the company went out of business before publication.

August 8, 2000, Chicago Sun-Times

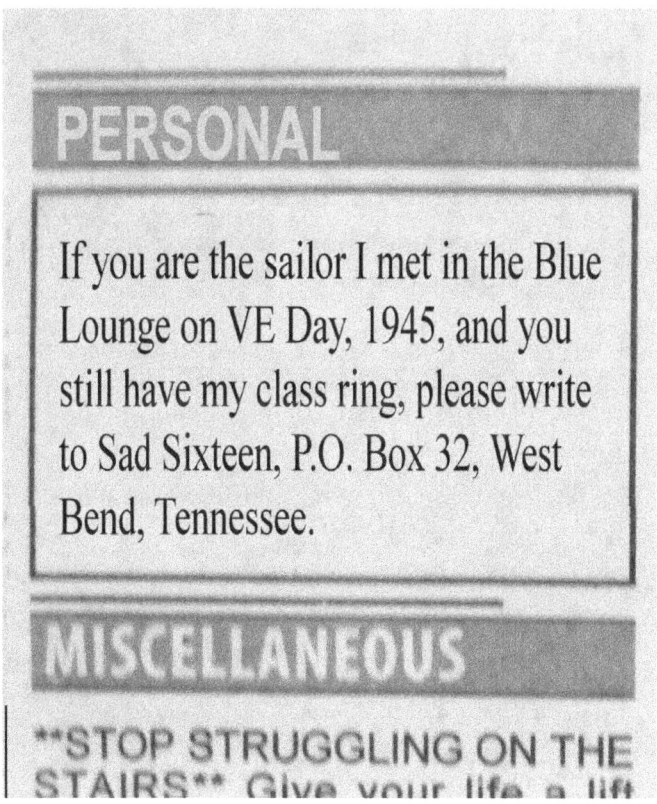

PERSONAL

If you are the sailor I met in the Blue Lounge on VE Day, 1945, and you still have my class ring, please write to Sad Sixteen, P.O. Box 32, West Bend, Tennessee.

MISCELLANEOUS

STOP STRUGGLING ON THE STAIRS Give your life a lift

August 20, 2000, Chicago Sun-Times

PERSONAL

Dear Sad Sixteen, Tennessee, eh?
I can't say I'm surprised. Whatever
made you think I'd still be in Chicago?
Well, I am. I'm 78 years young, and
can still cut a rug. How about you?
Sure, I have your ring. I've never
forgotten that night.
Seaman Henry (Butch) Randall

Will the party or parties responsible

August 20, 4:35 pm
sticky note on counter

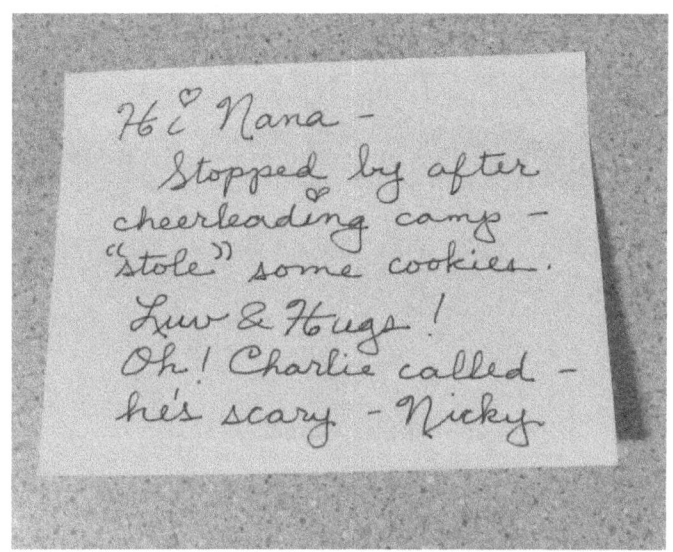

6:20 pm
newspaper lying on coffee table

Charlie — more threats
what to do? get a gun?
CANT do this much longer

Phone Memo

Call For: *Detective Kozlowski*

From	Company
Ms. Florence Anderson	

Date *August 21*	Time *8:02*		Phone
		a.m. ✓	( ) -
		p.m. ____	

Message *Grandson? Charles Adam Anderson continues*
to threaten violence if she doesn't give him more money.
Wants PPO? Wants permit to carry? Frightened. Please return call.

Action				Taken By
Phoned	Returned Your Call	Please Call Back	Will Call Again	*SCf*

POLICE INTERVIEW REPORT

| | official police use only |

Case No: 00-09-317   Date: Sept 1, 2000

Reporting Officer: Richard Kozlowski Prepared By: RK

Incident: Potential assault

transcript of taped interview

Person Making Complaint: Anderson, Florence Mrs.
Sex: F Race: Cau DOB: 4/12/1929
Address: 317 Honeysuckle Lane, West Bend, TN
Incident in Question: Potential Assault
Date of Incident: 8/20/2000 (and others unreported)
Time of Incident: 10:30 pm
Person(s) Involved: Charles Adam Anderson (great-grandson)
Witnesses with Direct Knowledge of this Incident: none
Description of Incident by Complainant: I was sitting in my
living room watching television when Charlie came in from the
kitchen. He knows where the key is for that door. He's been a
lot of trouble, and his daddy was too. He keeps after me to
give him money, but I don't have much at all, so he figured
out when my Social Security check comes, and started coming
by when he figured I'd have that. But I quit having the checks
sent to me, and now it goes right in my bank. So that makes
Charlie mad, because he can't get any money. But he's getting
worse- I think he's taking drugs, and this night he came in with
a gun. "Nana," he said (they all call me Nana), "I don't want
you lyin' to me any more. You got money in this house somewhere,
and you ain't needin' it like I am, so I want you to just get it
and give it to me."
I was scared silly, and that boy is just crazy. I don't have any
secret stash in my closet or anywheres. I guess he had enough
sense to know that if he shot me, I couldn't give him anything,
but what if he decides to come take the house apart? He won't find
anything and then he might just shoot me anyway.
I got other grandchildren, and great-grands too and they are all
good boys and girls. If he starts hurting them, we are all going
to be in a terrible way.

Signature of Complainant: *Florence Anderson*
(Mrs.) Florence Anderson

Departmental Response: Personal Protection Order Issued

Sep 1

Dear Butch —

How truly amazing that I've found you after all these years! My life has taken some interesting turns since we met so long ago. Soon after our memorable night, I met and married Freddie Anderson, whose family owned the garage here in West Bend. We moved down here the next winter. Freddie was so good to me! We raised a boy and two girls, but Freddie died in 1984 after a car fell on him.

Our Sandra and Diane are good girls, and they each have families of their own. Families are odd sometimes. Sandra married young, and had kids right away, while Diane was a few years younger, and she was a nurse, too, (an RN!) at the county hospital for quite a while till she met Stanley.

- 2 -

So, anyway, Sandra's grandson, Robert, and Diane's daughter, Nicky, are just a few months different in age. Diane married a man from Memphis (Stanley), but they live here now too, and they have a girl and a boy, Nicole (Nicky) and Alexander (Alex). They are the joys of my life. Alex just started playing Jr-hi football. He loves the mud! Nicky is a first-year cheerleader. She's all girl, but athletic too! They all call me Nana.

I'm not sure how to tell you about the oldest boy. He was born our first year, and he was trouble right from the start. His name is Ben, and it just seemed like no matter what Freddie and I did that Ben just couldn't make a good decision. He ran away when he was sixteen, but came back a

– 3 –

few years later with a trailer-
trash wife and a baby boy they
named Allen. That poor child
never really had a chance,
but somehow he managed to
graduate from high school despite
his daddy's drinking and yelling.
But it didn't seem to make much
difference, because he soon had
a baby boy too, and then Allen
ran away and left little Charlie
and his mama (Shelly) with nothing
but another old run-down trailer
and no money to live on. I
helped when I could when Charlie
was little, but you know, I was only
a candy striper way back in 1945,
and I never did make any big
money because I couldn't go to
school after I had my kids.
I worked hard and honest as

— 4 —

a nurse's aide, but no one would ever call me a "money bags," ha ha! Ben got himself killed in a bar fight in 1990, and Allen never did come back again, but the rest of the bunch all still live here.

I know this is all very complicated, and too many people for you to keep straight, but I wanted you to know how important my family is to me. And if we should meet again, you will hear lots more about them all.

I keep myself busy with garden club, and I do like to knit in the evenings while I watch TV.

What have you been doing with yourself?

For old times sake,
F lo (Sweet Sixteen)

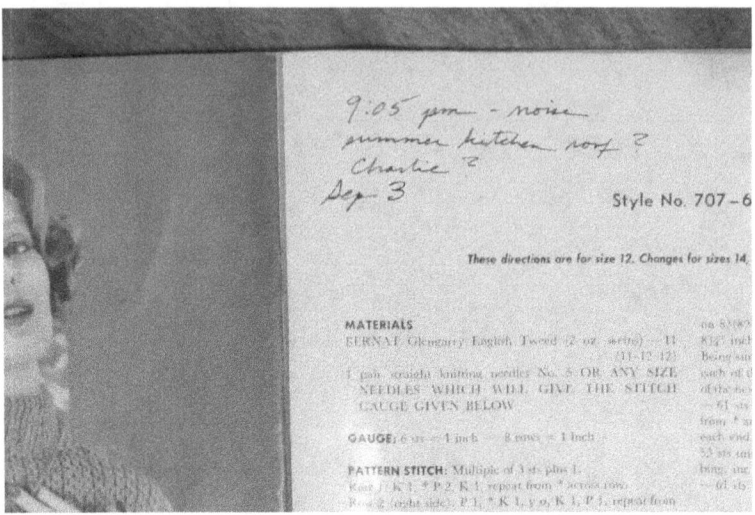

9:05 pm - noise
summer kitchen roof ?
Charlie ?
Sep 3

Style No. 707–6

These directions are for size 12. Changes for sizes 14,

MATERIALS
BERNAT Glengarry English Tweed (2 oz. skeins) — 11
(11–12–12)
1 pair straight knitting needles No. 5 OR ANY SIZE
NEEDLES WHICH WILL GIVE THE STITCH
GAUGE GIVEN BELOW

GAUGE: 6 sts = 1 inch   8 rows = 1 inch

PATTERN STITCH: Multiple of 3 sts plus 1.
Row 1: K 1, * P 2, K 1, repeat from * across row.
Row 2 (right side): P 1, * K 1, y o, K 1, P 1, repeat from

WEATHER
High 74, Low 49
Times of sun and clouds

West Bend Tattler

Wednesday
Sept 4, 2000
$1.00

Local Man Sought for Questioning

Police were called, shortly after 9 o'clock last night, to the home of Mrs. Florence Anderson, Honeysuckle Lane, after gunshots were reportedly heard. Mrs. Anderson, age 71, was knitting in the living room, while her grandchildren, Nicky and Alex Granger, were playing Monopoly in an upstairs bedroom. Mrs. Anderson claims to have heard scraping noises, after which she realized that someone was walking on the roof of the attached summer kitchen. She climbed the stairs to find out what her grandchildren were doing, but as she entered the spare bedroom, a shadow passed across the window, and several shots were fired.

No one was injured, and two bullets were recovered from the trunk of the large tulip tree in the yard. It is speculated that the incident was intended as a warning of some kind. The chief suspect is Mrs. Anderson's great-grandson, Charles Adam Anderson, also of West Bend. He is reputed to be a drug user.

The suspect's mother, Shelly Anderson, says she has not heard from Charles, but verifies that he owns a 22-caliber pistol. Police searched the premises, but neither the weapon nor the suspect was found.

A Personal Protection Order against Charles Anderson had been issued by the court just days ago, as a result of earlier threats he had made to Mrs. Anderson.

Weather Ideal for School Football

West Bend Central Sports
South Main St.
West Bend, TN

SOLD BY *J.K.H.*   DATE *9/5/00*

NAME *Diane Granger*

ADDRESS

CITY

☐ CASH ☒ CHARGE ☐ MDSE. RETD: PREVIOUS ▶
☐ C.O.D. ☐ PAID OUT ☐ PD' ON ACCT. BALANCE

*Order placed for two
"varsity" jackets,
West Bend colors,
1-SM, 1-M ,*

Order Received: phone

Visa (number on file)

Thank You!   RECEIVED BY

SEP 7

DEAR FLO —
How NICE TO HEAR
FROM YOU AGAIN! I GUESS
I SHOULD BRING YOU UP
TO DATE ON ME, TOO.
WELL, I MIGHT AS WELL
TELL YOU, I NEVER
AMOUNTED TO VERY MUCH.
I GOT A REAL BUM RAP
FROM THE NAVY. AFTER
OUR NIGHT TOGETHER,
YOU SEE, I MISSED MY
SHIP THE NEXT DAY, AND
GOT LISTED AS AWOL.
THERE WERE A BUNCH OF
US FELLOWS WHO DIDN'T
MAKE THE SAILING, BUT
THEY DECIDED TO MAKE
AN EXAMPLE OF ME.
IT'S A LONG STORY, BUT

2. I SPENT A FEW YEARS IN THE POKEY AND GOT A DISHONORABLE DISCHARGE. THAT'S WHAT OUR FUNNY GOVERNMENT WILL DO FOR A FELLER AFTER HE'S FOUGHT A WAR FOR THEM.

ANYWAY, I FINALLY ENDED UP DRIVING TRUCKS FOR 37 YEARS. I NEVER HAD ANY FAMILY, BUT I'VE BEEN AROUND.

I'M GLAD TO HEAR THAT YOU GOT SOME KIDS THAT TURNED OUT NICE, EVEN IF BEN WAS KIND OF A BLACK SHEEP. WHEN DID YOU SAY HE WAS BORN?

3.

ARE YOU SUGGESTING THAT YOU WOULD. LIKE TO RENEW OUR FRIEND- SHIP? I CAN STILL DRIVE CIRCLES AROUND ANYONE HALF MY AGE, AND I'D LOVE TO COME DOWN. AND VISIT IF YOU'RE AGREEABLE — YOU'RE ONLY ABOUT 8 HOURS FROM ME AND THIS TIME OF YEAR IS NICE. I'LL BRING THE RING.

FONDLY,

BUTCH
(HENRY RANDALL)

Sep 15

Dear Butch —

I would love to see you again! My life is quite simple, with no big engagements. Just let me know when you are coming. Do you like pot roast? Perhaps you should call. My number is 901-555-3408.

With anticipation,
Flo

BILL'S GUNS AND AMMO

Chicago Area Gun Show

Sept 25, 2000

sold to Henry Randall

9mm Glock pistol, 20 rounds ammo

price: $450.00 pd cash

1001

West Bend Junior High School
Student Incident Report

Student Involved _Alexander Granger_ Date of Incident _Oct 12, 2000_

Student's Grade _7_ Reported by _Peter Brown (coach)_

Details of Incident

Following football practice, Alex was approached by his older
cousin, Charlie Anderson (I think that's their relationship),
near the bleachers. Alex was putting on his new school
jacket, and Charlie grabbed him by both arms and began
yelling at him - something about the coat. Alex kept
insisting that his mother bought it, not "Nana,"
but Charlie apparently didn't believe this. Charlie said
(what I could hear), "If you and that ___ grandmother
of yours don't give me my share of the _____,
I'm gonna hurt you and your sister, too. I don't have to
stay away from you! Got it, stupid?"
Anderson then ran away down Elm St.

Action Taken: Police were called, morning of 10/13,
Charles Anderson known to be wanted for questioning.
Whereabouts at this time, unknown. It has been suggested
to Alex's parents that they pick him up from school.

Signature _P.P. Brown_

cc File   Revised 2017

187

October 13, 2000

gurry English Tweed (2 oz. skeins) — 11
(11-12-12)
knitting needles No. 5 OR ANY SIZE
WHICH WILL GIVE THE STITCH
/EN BELOW

= 1 inch   8 rows = 1 inch

H: Multiple of 3 sts plus 1.
P 2, K 1, repeat from * across row.
de): P 1, * K 1, y o, K 1, P 1, repeat from

P 3, K 1, repeat from * across ro
1, K 2, pass sl st over the 2 K
* across row.
ows for pattern

102/1
st at end
-121) sts
hes, ending
leg of each
n. Then work
hole dec), work
tog (armhole dec,
s, P 1, K 2. Being s
peat these 2 rows 6 t

on 83(89-95-101) sts until armholes measure 7¾(
8¼) inches, ending with Row 4. SHAPE SHOU
Being sure to dec the extra y o's of pattern st, at
each of the next 2 rows bind off 5(7-8-10) sts. A
of the next 2 rows bind off 6(7-9-10) sts, ending w
— 61 sts. NECKBAND: Row 1: P 1, * K 1, P
from * across row. Continue in K 1, P 1 ribbing
each end of n   every other row 4 times. Wor
53 sts up   d measures 3 inches. Contin
bind   nd of needle every other ro

d to back.

sts. K 1, P 1 in ri
edle on last row
1 st each end
ming new pa
92-96) sts u
'APE CAP
3 sts. Wo
attern
d 60(64

Butch called, Oh my!
I must be ready!
That SOB. Will be
here the night of
Alex's last game.
hope he likes
football.

oulder, neckband an
nd neckband in half and

October 26, 2000
sticky note on counter

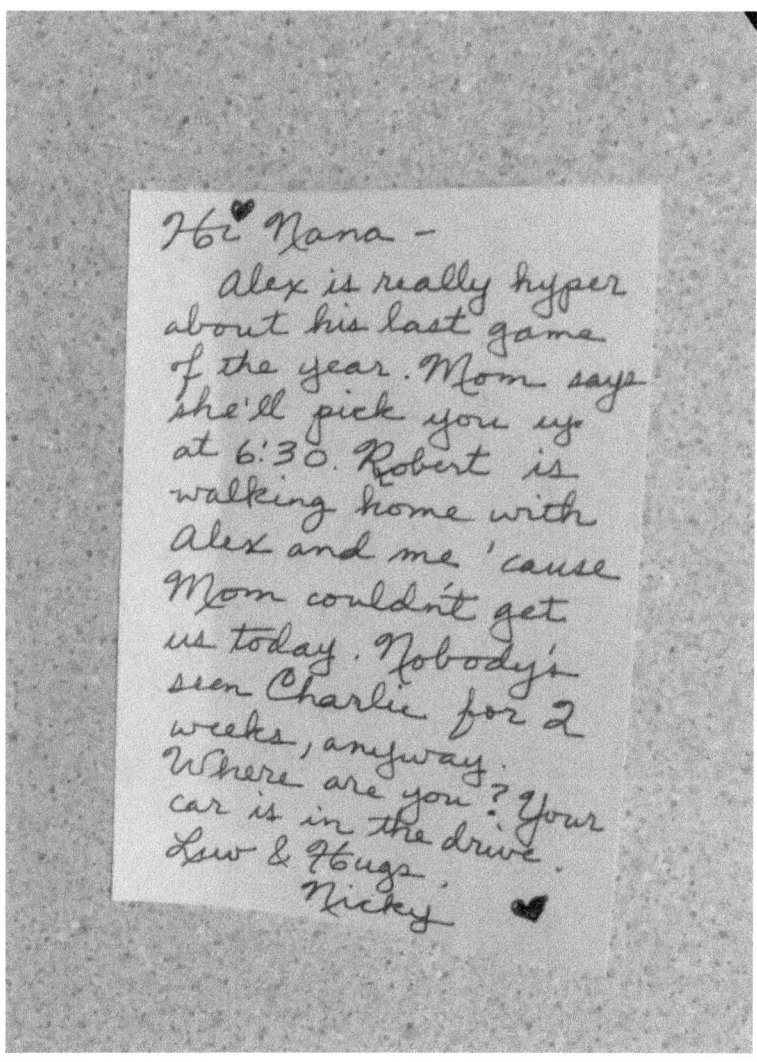

October 26, 2000
Granger front door

October 26, 2000 6:32 pm
Announcer at West Bend Jr-Hi Football Game

Ladies and gentlemen! Welcome to West Bend Memorial Stadium, and the final night of junior high football this season for the future Raider stars of West Bend, Tennessee! Let's hear it for our players as they enter the field. Here they come now, folks:

Number 14, Derek Mulligan at starting quarterback.

Center tonight will be Harvey Smith, number 74.

At Left Tackle, number 62, Alex Granger.

Playing Right Tackle, number 65...

Wait. Ladies and gentlemen, we have some confusion on the field. Alex Granger seems to have fallen, and I'm being told that there was the sound of shots. He's moving, O God, thank God, he's moving, ladies and gentlemen... I apologize, but this is extraordinary. Has someone called 911?

He's being carried off the field to the bench. They are wrapping his leg in a towel, and there appears to be blood seeping out around his ankle. I think perhaps we can conclude that whatever has happened to Alex is not life threatening.

Ladies and Gentlemen, I'm sure you can hear the sirens, the police are arriving. I suggest that you all take your seats and we will... we will attempt to... begin the game just as soon as possible. The ambulance seems to be arriving, also. But... wait... it's not coming onto the field, but is stopping near the entrance. We seem to have two people down over there. Does anyone understand what's happening?

[voice slightly muffled] What? Where? No. Out there too?

Mr. Cunnningham. Mr. Cunningham! Can we call upon you to have the band play a few numbers until we can determine if the game may yet be played... Yes, I see your wave. Thank you. Let's give a big hand for our West Bend Raiders Junior High Band!

WEST BEND EMT SERVICE - PATIENT REPORT

SERVICE NAME / VEHICLE#		SERVICE #		INCIDENT #			TODAY'S DATE
Lifeline Ambulance		37		14			10 26 00

INCIDENT LOCATION					TRANSPORTED TO	
West Bend High School					County Memorial	

PATIENT LAST NAME	FIRST		M.I.		AGE	Gender	DATE OF BIRTH
unknown					75 ?	M	

PATIENT ADDRESS		CITY		STATE	ZIP

CHIEF COMPLAINT

Medications	☐ Pt. States None	☐ Unknown	☐ Brought W/Pt.	List:

ALLERGIES	☐ Pt. States None	☐ Unknown	List:

MEDICAL HISTORY	☐ Pt. States None	☐ Unknown	☐ Asthma	☐ Cardiac	☐ COPD	☐ Renal Failure	☐ Seizure
	☐ Stroke/CVA	☐ Cancer	☐ CHF	☐ Diabetes	☐ Htn	☐ Other	

Patient Signs

L.O.C.	SPEECH	SKIN	COLOR	RESPIRATION	PULSE	PUPILS	Call Received
__Alert	__Coherent	X Normal	__Normal	__Normal	__Normal	__Reactive L / R	6:33
__Voice	__Incoherent	__Moist	__Cyanotic	__Rales	__Rapid	__Dialated L / R	
__Pain	__Slurred	__Hot	__Pale	X Distressed	__Slow	X Equal	Dispatch
X Unrespon	X Silent	__Cool	__Flushed	__Absent	__Absent	__Unequal	6:34
					weak & thready		

Medical Condition

					On Scene
__Abdominal Pain	__Pediactric Cardiac Arrest	__Coma	__Near Drowning	__Stroke	6:45
__A.M.S.	__Cardiac Chest Pains	__Fx / Disloc.	__Poisons / OD	__Suspect Spinal Inj	
__Amputation	__Cardiac Dysrhythmias	__Head Trauma	__Eclampsia / Pre	__Syncope	In Service
__Anaphylaxis	__Ped. Dysrhythmias	__Hyperthermia	X Resp Distress	__Vaginal Bleeding	7:30
__Burns	__Childbirth	__Hypoglycemia	__Seizures	__Death in the Field	
__Cardiac Arrest	__Congestive Heart Failure	__Hypothermia	X Shock	__General Patient Care	

TIME	B / P	P	Resp.	TREATMENT
6:48	90/80	37	9	

Patient Assisted Medications		MEDICATIONS GIVEN	
Nitroglycerin __		QTY. DOSE	
Auto inhaler __		__ __ Glucose Paste	
Auto Injection Epinephrine __		__ __ Charcoal	

NARRATIVE

small diameter puncture wound entering below rib cage and extending upwards.
Knitting needle inserted in the wound. Removal at scene not attempted.
Stabilized and transported.

Transferred to County Medical ER at 7:12

REFUSAL OF TREATMENT / TRANSPORT

This is to certify that I am refusing Treatment / Transport and have been informed of the risks of doing so.

X_____ _____

Patient Signature Date/Time

X_____ _____

Witness Signature Date/Time

Crew Member # 1	EMS License #	Crew Member # 3	EMS License #
Crew Member # 2	EMS License #	Crew Member # 4	EMS License #

Joan H. Young

EMERGENCY MEDICAL SERVICES (EMS)
PATIENT CARE WORKSHEET

This form is for use by ambulance service providers who are unable to immediately comply with Chapters HFS 10, 11, 12 ar apply to documentation of ambulance runs by completing and providing patient care information to the receiving facility when the Per the above administrative rules, this form becomes part of the patient's medical record.

INSTRUCTIONS: Print legibly. Complete all sections of this worksheet. A copy of this worksheet or the ambular completed and left with the receiving facility when the patient is delivered. This form does not constitute the officia care report.

Ambulance Service: Harlan Funeral Home~ alternate trans. for multi-victim casualty **Run**

Incident Date: Oct 26, 2000   **Incident Location:** West Bend football fiel

Patient Name: Florence Anderson, as identified by her daughter Diane Granger

DOB _____ **Age:** 70   **Sex:** ☐ Male ☒ Female   **W**

Patient Address: _____

Chief Complaint: close range G S W to thorax

Physician: _____

NOI / MOI: _____

GCS: Eyes 4-1 _____ Speech 5-1 _____ Motor 6-1 _____ To

LOC: Alert X (Check one) ☐ 1 ☐ 2 ☐ 3   (Check all that apply) ☐ Respond to verb
                                                                ☒ Unres

Time	BP	Pulse Rate / Quality	Respiratory Rate	Oximetry	Glu
6:47	0 /0	0	0		

Skin: (Check all that apply) ☐ Warm ☐ Dry ☐ Moist ☐ Cold ☐ Flush ☒ Pa

Eyes: (Check all that apply) ☐ PERRL ☐ Constricted ☐ Dilated ☒ Non-reactive

O₂ Given: ☐ Yes ☒ No   **Rate of flow:** _____ (Check one) ☐ Mask

Allergies: _____ **Last Oral Intake:** ____

Medications: _____

Past Medical History (Check all that apply) ☐ Cardiac ☐ CHF ☐ Hypertension ☐ Seizure ☐ Diabetes

   Other _____

Treatment: pronounced dead at scene at 6:47 p.m.

EMERGENCY MEDICAL SERVICES (EMS)
PATIENT CARE WORKSHEET

This form is for use by ambulance service providers who are unable to immediately comply with Chapters HFS 10, 11, 12 ar apply to documentation of ambulance runs by completing and providing patient care information to the receiving facility when th Per the above administrative rules, this form becomes part of the patient's medical record.

INSTRUCTIONS: Print legibly. Complete all sections of this worksheet. A copy of this worksheet or the ambular completed and left with the receiving facility when the patient is delivered. This form does not constitute the officia care report.

Ambulance Service: Harlan Funeral Home— alternate trans. for multi-victim casualty **Run**

Incident Date: Oct 26, 2000   **Incident Location:** West Bend football fiel

Patient Name: identified as Charlie Anderson by husband of cousin, Stanley Granger

DOB _____ **Age:** late teens **Sex:** [X] Male ☐ Female   **W**

Patient Address: _____

Chief Complaint: close range GSW to thorax

Physician: _____

NOI / MOI: _____

GCS: Eyes 4-1 _____ Speech 5-1 _____ Motor 6-1 _____ Tᴏ
LOC: Alert X (Check one) ☐ 1 ☐ 2 ☐ 3   (Check all that apply) ☐ Respond to verb
                                                    [X] Unres

Time	BP	Pulse Rate / Quality	Respiratory Rate	Oximetry	Glu
6:49	0/0	0	0		

Skin: (Check all that apply) ☐ Warm ☐ Dry ☐ Moist ☐ Cold ☐ Flush [X] Pᴀ

Eyes: (Check all that apply) ☐ PERRL ☐ Constricted ☐ Dilated [X] Non-reactive

O₂ Given: ☐ Yes [X] No   **Rate of flow:** _____ (Check one) ☐ Mask

Allergies: _____   **Last Oral Intake:** ___

Medications: _____
Past Medical History (Check all that apply) ☐ Cardiac ☐ CHF ☐ Hypertension ☐ Seizure ☐ Diabetes
    Other _____

Treatment: pronounced dead at scene at 6:50

194

Joan H. Young

COUNTY HOSPITAL
ER ADMISSIONS

NAME ___Alexander Granger___ DATE OF ADMISSION __Oct 26, 2000__
DATE OF BIRTH __12/1/88__ SEX __M__ MARITAL STATUS __-__ CHILDREN __-__
RESIDENCE ____
OCCUPATION __student__ NATIVITY ____ RELIGION ____

ADMINISTRATION
NEXT OF KIN/GUARDIAN __Diane Granger - Mother__ TEL. ____
PERSONAL PHYSICIAN ____ TEL. ____
AGENT (IF ANY) ____ TEL. ____
REGISTER NUMBER ____ WARD __214__ BED __2__ CARE NOTE ____

HISTORY
MODE OF { VOLUNTARY __Mother transported__ CERTIFIED ____
ADMISSION { TRANSFER FROM ____ CRIMINAL ____

PULSE __80__ BLOOD PRESSURE __120/84__ RESPIRATION __14__ TEMPERATURE __98.2__
MENTAL STATE ON ADMISSION ____

SUPPOSED CAUSES - PREDISPOSING __through and through GSW to right calf__

EXCITING ____

PHYSICAL CONDITION __stable, wound cleaned and dressed, admitted for observation__
__transferred to room 214 at 1146 pm__

SPECIAL CIRCUMSTANCES ____

WEATHER
High 74, Low 49
Times of sun and clouds

West Bend Tattler

Friday
Oct 27, 2000
$1.00

Triple Muder Motives Unclear

Fans of the Junior High football playoffs were astonished last night to witness a triple homicide. Despite the presence of several hundred people, the exact details of the sequence of events are elusive.

Lead Detective Richard Kazlowski stated that it is clear the incident began when Charles Adam Anderson shot his cousin (first cousin once removed), Alexander Granger, in the leg. It is speculated at press time that Anderson was jealous of his cousin who is a starter on the football team, and who recently received an expensive school jacket as a gift from a family member. Various team members readily admitted that they had seen Charlie threaten Alex, apparently in reference to the jacket.

Granger is reported to be resting comfortably at County Memorial Hospital, and a full recovery is expected.

Two of the three fatalities are also members of the Anderson family. Charles Adam Anderson, age 17, of West Bend was pronounced dead at the scene, as was Florence Anderson, age 71. Florence is the grandmother of Alex Granger, and great-grandmother of Charles. Her death is the result of a gunshot wound to the chest, at close range, presumed to have been delivered by the third victim.

The identity of this third person has tentatively been established as Henry Randall, of Chicago, Illinois. His relationship to the victims is not known, although witnesses say that he and Florence Anderson entered the stadium together. Randall died early this morning at County Memorial of a puncture wound which ruptured his aorta. Emergency surgery was performed, but repairs to the vessel were unsuccessful. He did not regain consciousness.

Detective Kowalski stated that it is early for conclusions, but apparently Charles Anderson shot his cousin Alex. Realizing what had occurred, Randall pulled a Glock 9mm handgun from his jacket and shot Charles. It is speculated that Florence Anderson, distraught at this violence to her great-grandson, removed a knitting needle from her tote bag and stabbed Randall, whereupon Randall turned the gun on his companion before collapsing.

Since all parties are deceased, no charges are being filed.

The football game is rescheduled for this coming week.

196

found on May 20, 2009 by Nicole Granger Stokes while looking
through a box of her grandmother's knitting pattern books

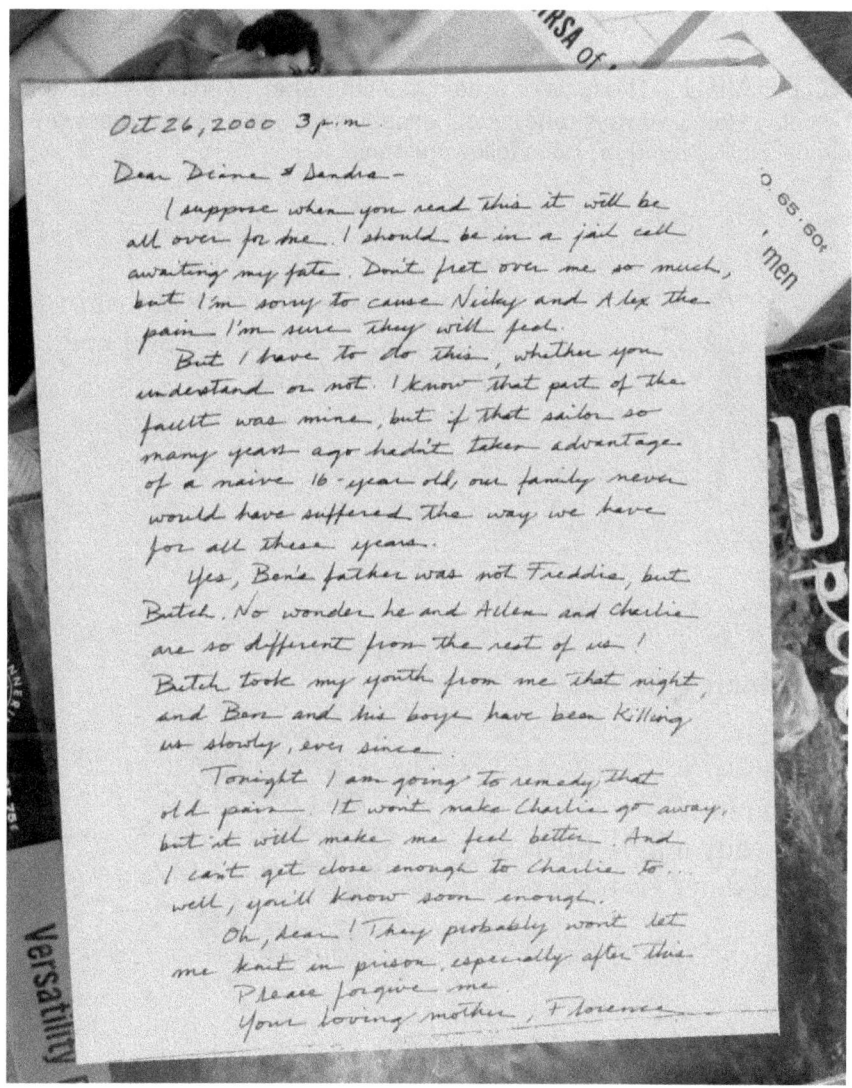

Spruce Spear

NOT HAIKU – These were written at a time when everyone seemed to be doing Haiku. Always rebellious, I experimented with poems that were almost Haiku, but don't quite follow the rules.

Spruce spear piercing sky-skin.
Pour, bleed maple red and gold.
September death.

Madame October

Fading lady
With your maple lipstick
smeared across a granite
face.

A Golden Chip of Sunshine
38 - February 23, 1999

NON-FICTION – This is a chapter excerpted from the book *North Country Cache*, a collection of essays about my adventures hiking the North Country Trail. The book took third place in Regional Non-fiction from Independent Publishers in 2005.

Chips is pulling on his leash with his usual imperative exuberance, nearly forcing me to jog to keep up with him. It's a gray and overcast Tuesday, but we have traveled just a few miles from home to walk some trail that I have not yet seen.

My little golden dog, I cherish the memories of you as a ball of fluff, an exceptionally beautiful puppy. You were just 12 weeks old when I rolled a ball for you and you immediately brought it back. I added the word "fetch," and there was your favorite game! In my mind I see you running towards me, a half-grown puppy, your red rubber ball held in your mouth.

With a "snap" the clip on Chips' leash breaks loose from his collar, and I decide to let him run free for a while. Enthusiastically, he ranges back and forth across the trail searching for some extra-interesting smell to follow.

Puppy Chips enjoying a canoe ride

You are such a bright light in my life! Your puppy fur was a glistening white gold, the color of fresh split maple chips... and so you were named "Chips." I know you are so attached to me that you cry and pout whenever I am forced to leave you behind on some expedition, whether it's just a ride to the Post Office, or a hike where dogs are not welcome. And I know that I am equally attached to you. When we are together you love to rest your head in my lap, and I welcome your doggy kisses. You abandon yourself in telling me how much you love me.

We reach a downed tree, spreading its branches rudely across the trail. With no problem at all, Chips jumps across the large horizontal trunk.

"Ready for Adventure" is your life's motto. At four months of age you took to riding on the bow of my canoe. When you discovered long hikes with us, you embraced the outdoor life with an intensity equal to mine. Only once in the more than 1200 miles of North Country Trail that you have hiked with us did you question the request to come have your pack put on. And we could hardly blame you on that 105° North Dakota day! You learned to ride in my pack, and climb ladders with never a look back. Sharing one sleeping bag on cold nights keeps us both warm and happy. You are entertained for hours with nothing but a stick and a human to throw it for you.

The sun breaks through the clouds briefly, but there is no sunshine in my heart today.

How can Dr. Jim be right? How can what he told me on Thursday be true, that you have only six months to live? I know that Jim is trying to break the news to me gently, so I realize that we've probably only got three months left together. Jim says you have a tumor the size of a football inside your rib cage, that it weighs almost ten pounds. The five pounds you have lost, which prompted me to take you to the doctor, are actually more like ten pounds of muscle and healthy organs. But you seem so normally energetic, just a little thin...

Joan H. Young

Chips barks eagerly at an elusive squirrel, and we turn around to head back toward the car. The brown leaves are crunchy beneath my feet with only a light dusting of snow – easy walking for me, and easy tracking of interesting smells for a curious dog. We need to return home in time for Chips to eat before noon, so that his stomach will be empty for his surgery tomorrow morning.

Should I put you through this trauma, dear pup? Jim says the tumor is in your liver and that there is really nothing that can be done, but his partner, Dr. Paul, thinks it might be in the spleen. He says spleen tumors can be huge and still be removed successfully. Jim says that the surgery may shorten your life, that you might not even survive it. But to do nothing to try to save you is not a choice I can live with.

At home, Chips eats some dog chow and then I pour the rest of the food from his dish back into the bag. He gives me a look of total surprise at this strange turn of events. "What the heck?" he clearly asks. It's a funny scene, but I wish I hadn't caused him even this minor insult when tomorrow may be his last day. I can see that the mass inside him has shifted back a little, into his abdomen, making him look slightly pregnant.

Wednesday morning at the veterinary office Jim draws blood from Chips to do a liver function test. He puts Chips in a kennel to wait, and lets me sit in the cement and chain-link room with him. We will not tolerate separation now. Chips sprawls, flattening his tummy on the cool cement, shunning a warmer and softer mat provided for comfort.

Are your insides on fire, my Chiplet? You have always been on fire with the joy of life. Remember when I had to walk you eight miles to even tire you out as a six-month-old puppy? Remember all the hours of retrieving sticks thrown in lakes or rivers? You love that even more than your ball. And that ball! How many times have you leapt in the air to catch a ball thrown high before it could bounce even one time? I always thought you would break your teeth catching that hard rubber toy that way, but you never did.

201

I know that Jim will do everything he can to save you. If you die during surgery, so be it. At least there will be no long sad end.

At last Jim returns and calls us into the examination room. The liver function tests are done. The news is not good. The values are off the chart by which they evaluate such things. Jim explains that this means that the liver is fully involved and there is no way he can survive major surgery, because the liver is responsible for de-toxification after the anaesthetic. "Take him home and enjoy what time you have left, Joan," Jim says gently. This often gruff, but always caring, vet has helped me through the deaths of several dogs, but there has never been a dog like Chips before.

Your middle name may be Houdini, but I don't think you are going to be able to escape this sentence, my furry friend. You can slip any collar or harness. You can wriggle through a car window opened only a few inches. No fence has ever kept you cooped up for long. Remember the day that you escaped Phil's back yard? We wouldn't have believed it if we hadn't watched you pull the pin in the gate latch with your teeth, flip the latch and then open the gate. But there's no latch on this door that is closing today.

Thursday morning, Chips is not nestled in bed with me when I awake. He is spread-eagled on the bathroom floor, trying to cool the hot monster in his belly. When he stands up I can see that the tumor has grown, overnight. He now looks pear-shaped. I give him food and water, but whatever he eats or drinks comes right back up. I tempt him with his favorites, cheese and milk. Nothing stays down. Despite the facts presented to me over the past six days, the finality of the truth that my dog is dying smashes into me, and all I can do is watch and wonder how long it will take.

Baby dog, I wish you would eat just a little bit. If you won't even have some milk you are surely in trouble. You've been my Dairy Dog, the Parmezan Pup, the Yogurt Yipper. Ice cream, yogurt, cheese and milk have always had you drooling near my knee, your tail twitching with anticipation as you wait for a treat.

Thursday evening, Chips lies on his back on the couch, a favorite position, while I rub his tummy and chin. It doesn't feel right, with that hard lump filling all that space that should be so soft, but he seems to derive some comfort from my touch.

Sharing a special moment

You've always insisted on being close enough to touch me, haven't you? You lie beneath my desk while I work, your head resting across my foot. In the car you know you can't sit in my lap while I drive, but you have to have either the tip of your nose or a paw, just making contact with my thigh across the center console. When you first left your litter-mates, and we made that first long drive to Ann Arbor together, you felt calm and safe as long as I rested one hand on your fuzzy back. Does my touch calm you at all today, when I am anything but calm?

At about ten o'clock Chips begins to wag his tail in an odd manner, not rhythmically, but in a jerking motion. He walks around in a few circles, and jumps on the couch to be held. His heart is racing in an unnatural manner. The look on his face is one of utter surprise. In about five minutes, his heart settles back to a normal rhythm, but the attack has done its work; he's clearly weaker now.

How can you be so weak just two days after our walk in the woods when you must have roamed 15 miles to my eight? You are such a strong dog... pulling with such strength for your 40 pounds that grown men have wondered aloud at your power. Such statements have usually been preceded by teasing me for barely being able to control such a small dog. Then after taking you for a walk themselves they would return and exclaim profound truths such as, "You weren't kidding... this dog is STRONG!"

During the night Chips retches nearly every hour. Each episode is followed by a deep agonizing groan, which sounds as if it is tearing his insides apart. Each groan tears at my heart, but there is nothing I can do except try to keep him comfortable. He now wants only to stay on the floor where it is cooler. I had thought he would become less conscious of what was happening as the end came nearer, but such relief is not to be.

You are looking at me with those wonderful liquid eyes, asking questions I cannot answer. You are clearly saying, "I don't understand." And neither do I, my Baby Dog. All I can promise you is no more leashes, fences, and choke collars. There will be meadows and woods in which to run free in the sun, and to feel the wind in your ears. Remember Heze? He was old when you were a puppy and was grumpy when you chewed on his ears, but now he will welcome you. Get acquainted with Butchy-Boy and Charlotte, Bonnie, Billie and all the others who have gone before you. You find us some good trails to follow, and wait for me.

This can not go on. If Chips is still alive when Jim's office opens, I will take him in, and make the end more bearable for both of us.

At 5:35 in the morning, Chips gives one horrible groan, arches his back, and goes limp. The light fades from his eyes; his heart is not beating.

Goodbye, my golden Chip of sunshine.

4 miles this hike
Freesoil Rd. to 5-Mile Rd.
Lake County, MI
1180 total NCT miles

A Blue Rubber Ball

A blue rubber ball
Hidden in the stubbled field...
When did you lose it, my
Golden Chip of Sunshine?

It was well-chewed,
Had played hard, like you.
Did you laugh when you dropped it,
Thinking to tease?

Ten years and more
The grasses have hidden it.
How swift are the shadows
That measure our days.

A red rubber ball
Nestled with your buried bones...
Do you run the forever fields
Awaiting another game?

Slugging it Out on Jimmerson Hill

HUMOR - This country song was written as we hiked the hills of Western New York, as told in the book, *North Country Cache*.

We don't wash our white sink
Until it turns brown.
So we left our homes for Olean
Where the oil seeps from the ground.
Some folks say we're crazy,
But we know we're O.K.
Hiking to the Genesee
From Allegheny, P.A.

The hills they are Jim-Dandy,
Like stairways to the sky.
We're having fun in the summer sun,
But we have to wonder why!
Moaning thighs and aching backs
Our lungs and knees give way,
Hiking to the Genesee
From Allegheny, P.A.

We greet the slugs at breakfast,
We race them all day long.
We hike and smile for many a mile,
While they just slime along.
Every night they meet us,
They sing this ron-do-lay:
[next two lines to be sung falsetto]
We beat you to the Genesee
From Allegheny, P.A.

We've seen fantastic sights
Like the stream where Sunfish Run.
We heard the Hencoop Holler,
And the Dog was Lichen some fun.
If you're in Hungry Hollow
There's Mutton just over the way,
Hiking to the Genesee
From Allegheny, P.A.

The Valley

LITERARY FICTION – This story first appears in the *3288 Review*, a literary journal published by Caffeinated Press.

She stumbled into the valley as dusk was fading into night. It was the wrong trail but that hardly mattered now. There was a clear treadway snaking between two boulders; the path glowed paler in the moonlight than the rocks and forest litter beneath the dark trees, and she just wanted to get somewhere. Somewhere safe.

Her pack scraped against the rough stone, distracting her as she twisted to free the buckle that had snagged on a sapling struggling for life in a crevice. *If only I was thinner,* she thought. She had to unclip the straps to free herself. When she finally lifted her gaze to look ahead, her breath caught in her throat.

At least a dozen figures stood in a ragged horseshoe around the end of a pond that glowed faintly, as if there were some silvery phosphorescent life form teeming just below the surface of the water. Shrubs laden with white berries surrounded the pool, highlighting its oval shape.

The figures were clothed similarly in some kind of hooded diaphanous robe. She couldn't even tell who was male or female, or if perhaps they were androgynous.

Angels? A cult?

One person with a slight build, dressed in everyday cargo shorts and a t-shirt, with short hair, stood on a flat rock at the open end of the horseshoe. He or she squirmed nervously, but then focused on the pool, looking straight ahead.

The group began to hum, and slowly raised their arms in

unison. The higher their arms, the more focused became the lone sacrifice—that's what the person on the end looked like.

A single moonbeam shot through some opening in the leafy canopy and spread slightly in a white ray connecting the heavens with the surface of the pond. The outstretched arms lifted higher and the hum became louder.

Suddenly, as if in response to the light and sound and arms lifted to their highest, the one person who looked like an ordinary human being bent its knees and dove into the pool.

She was so shocked, she gasped.

Bodies turned, and a dozen pairs of eyes focused on her.

At least they're human eyes. But even in the bright moonlight she couldn't assess their mood.

In the next moment that mystical first impression was shattered as several of the people rushed toward her, arms outstretched in welcoming gestures. She felt no fear, only relief. Her hand went, unconsciously, to her forehead, and her fingers came away wet. She stared stupidly at the dark stain. The crusty first scab must have rubbed against that stone when she was struggling with her pack.

"Come," someone urged. A woman's voice. "Let me look at that cut."

A gentle crush of bodies surrounded her, touching her arms and shoulders, supporting her as they guided her toward a cluster of metal and nylon lawn chairs. Someone lifted the pack from her back. It had been hanging on her shoulders since she'd unclipped the hip belt up at that rocky entrance to this valley. She could now see that the pool was centered at the bottom of a broad bowl with wooded slopes. Off to the side, the coals of a banked fire glowed red, and beyond that stood a assemblage of assorted tents.

It was a relief to have the pack weight gone, and she lowered herself into one of the seats. Some of the members of the group sat and others remained standing. She touched her head again, smearing a new rivulet of blood.

"It's really nothing," she protested. "I fell earlier and banged my forehead on a jagged tree stump. But I'm lost and hungry. Do you know how to get back to the main trail?"

"Yes, I think we can help you with that tomorrow," said a deeper voice.

The woman who had said, "Come," pushed back her hood, revealing a kind face haloed in the moonlight with soft gray hair. She held a damp washcloth in her hand. "May I?" She smiled and placed a hand on the seated woman's head, as if pronouncing a blessing.

"Of course." The cloth was warm.

"You're a long way from the path most of the hikers follow," the woman said as she gently washed the cut.

"I...I was with a group, but we got separated." She wondered how much she should tell them.

"They'll be looking for you then," said another voice. "Do you have a cell phone? Maybe you should you let them know you're all right. But you'll have to go back up the path a ways to get reception."

Although these people were complete strangers, and the trail that led between the large rocks which the man pointed toward was familiar, a sudden tremor of fear passed through her at the thought of leaving this comforting circle of human companionship.

"You can stay with us for the night after you call. We'll find some extra blankets." This voice came from the edge of the group, another woman.

"No, please. I don't want to talk to them," she protested. Now she'd have to tell. Any normal person would want to reassure her friends.

"I'm just going to turn on this flashlight for a minute to make sure I've got that wound cleaned out," the first woman said. "My name is Michaela."

"I'm Fritz," said the man who had told her he could take her back to the main trail.

"Oh, I'm Kaimi, K-A-I-M-I," she responded. "Just say Kami. My parents liked weird spellings." She squeezed her eyes shut as a light was switched on. She could feel the beam playing over her face and eyelids.

"That's all right then," Michaela said. She turned out the penlight and pulled a large Band-Aid from her pocket. "You were right. It doesn't look too bad. But we wouldn't want it to get infected."

Fritz pulled his chair closer and asked, "What happened to you?"

There wasn't much use in trying to hide the truth. Anything she could make up would sound even stupider than reality.

"We had a fight, and..." she began, but her voice trailed off.

"Ah, that explains some things," Fritz said softly. "But weren't you concerned about going off alone?"

Kaimi looked at him. He, too, had removed his hood. He was a regular looking guy. Thin, with brown hair pulled back into a pony tail and a curly beard. He cocked his head to the side and his dark eyes twinkled.

"I was so mad, I didn't care," she admitted. "My friends—she said this word in a sarcastic tone—told me I was too fat to be a real hiker. They said they'd only brought me on this trip so there would be one more person to help carry the gear, but if I couldn't keep up, they'd just let me find the campsite on my own."

"They don't sound like very good friends," said the woman who had offered her a blanket. "I'm Muriel, by the way."

"Well, they were right," Kaimi said bitterly. "I couldn't even find the right trail on my own."

Fritz looked thoughtful. "Who's to say which trail is correct? It all depends on where you want to go."

Kaimi laughed. "I think you stole that line from the Cheshire Cat."

"Perhaps," Fritz laughed too. "But he was a wise cat."

A giggling girl placed a small, cool basket in her lap. "I wove it myself. I'm just learning how," she added.

Kaimi looked down and saw an uneven shallow cup made of cattail leaves, filled with bread and cheese. It looked elfin, except for the commercial energy bar nestled beside the cheddar squares.

Another man slipped a travel mug into the holder in the arm of the chair. "Here's fresh tea," he said. "You must need some nourishment."

"Thanks. Yes, the worst of it is, my friends have all the food. But I have the stove and a lot of the tools. They might make fun of me for being chubby, but I'm pretty sure they had to eat a cold supper tonight." Small vengeful thoughts sparkled at the edges of Kaimi's mind, but they seemed to fizzle out in the presence of her new acquaintances. Suddenly, she felt sorry for her former "friends" and had a strange desire to be desperately honest. "I lost my water bottle," she confessed. "That's my own dumb fault. A hot drink will be really nice." She sipped the mug of tea and ate a chunk of cheese.

The girl who had given her the food asked, "Do you want to sleep in my tent? I'm Angela."

Kaimi suddenly felt wary once more. "I have a tent and my own sleeping bag, thanks. I'll just set up beside your camp."

And where was the person who had gone in the water? Everyone she could see was wearing one of those strange robes—she could almost see through them, but not quite. No one looked wet.

After she had eaten, she said, "I'm really tired. If you don't mind, I'll just pitch my tent and crawl in the sack."

"Your castle awaits," Fritz said. He bowed with a touch of mock chivalry and gestured toward the shadowing nylon village.

Kaimi turned and saw that someone had set up her tent.

"Thanks, you've... you've all been so nice. And you don't even know me." she stammered.

Muriel smiled. "We're happy to welcome those who find our campsite."

Kaimi awoke refreshed and hungry. She could smell the campfire and bacon, but she lay quietly in her sleeping bag, wondering about these campers. They seemed otherworldly and ordinary all at the same time. *Are they trustworthy? How long have they been here?* The sun was high enough to warm the air and make leaf shadows dance on the nylon tent. Insects buzzed.

The girl who had given her food last night—*was her name Angela?*—spoke outside the tent. "If you're awake, there's coffee or hot chocolate. And bacon and eggs."

Soon she was again seated in one of the lawn chairs balancing a tin plate full of delicious food. The coffee was strong and she inhaled its strengthening aroma before drinking.

Is this a permanent campsite? she wondered. *There's nothing really heavy here, like a picnic table, but this is a lot of stuff to carry in by hand. And I don't see anywhere a vehicle could drive in.*

Fritz came and sat beside her.

"Don't you think you should let your friends know you are all right, or family?" he began.

"I suppose," Kaimi agreed reluctantly. *What if they come back looking for me? I don't want them to take me away.*

Michaela brought a chair over and settled in with her own mug of coffee.

"How are you feeling this morning?" she asked.

"Much better, thank you. The food is great. Are you sure you have enough to share?"

Michaela smiled. "Of course! We don't actually live here, but we keep our coolers well stocked. That pond is spring fed, and if we keep them submerged we don't even need ice." She changed the topic. "How's your head?"

Kaimi touched the bandage. "It doesn't hurt at all. I almost forgot," she laughed.

"And you aren't hurt anywhere else?" Michaela prompted.

"Oh, no!" Kaimi assured her. *Except for my soul. Where did that come from?*

Michaela reached out and touched Kaimi's knee. "You just let us know if there's anything we can help with. Let me take your plate. Did you have enough food?"

Kaimi nodded.

Fritz stood and said, "Let's walk up the trail and make a call. Does your phone have enough juice left?"

"I think so," Kaimi answered.

Now that she was out here on the other side of that
narrow doorway through the split rock, the forest didn't look as
threatening as it had yesterday in the gloom of late evening.
Clearly, the trail she'd been on followed a ridge, and she could
hardly imagine how she'd wandered down the slope to the
campsite in the valley. *If I hadn't found these people, I'd be
really hungry right now.*

They climbed slowly but steadily to a height of land with
a small clearing. But there was no view; it was ringed with
trees. Suddenly, she wondered if it had been wise to come out
here alone with a man she hardly knew.

But Fritz didn't seem to be treating her any differently
from the way he had in the presence of the others. "This is
where most cell phones can get a signal," he said, stroking his
beard.

Kaimi pulled her phone out of her pocket and turned it
on. She pointed at it. "Two bars, but the power is really low.
My friends will still be in the woods, but I can call my mom
and let her know I'm safe."

"Good idea."

She punched in the numbers and the call went to
voicemail. Kaimi was secretly glad. She didn't really want to
make any connection with her family. This trip was supposed
to be a chance to get away and evaluate her life. At the beep
she said, "Hi, Mom. I'm just calling to tell you I've met some
new friends in the woods, and I'm camping with them for a few
days. I'll call again when I get home." She disconnected
quickly, in case her mother might actually be there, and pick
up.

Fritz raised an eyebrow. "A few days?"

Kaimi looked sheepish. "If it's all right. I mean... my
original trip was going to last a week. The friends I was with,
from school, just think I'm a loser anyway. I can pay you for
the food I eat."

"No need for that. How will you get home?"

"If you show me the main trail, I can hike back to where
we started and bum a ride. That's shorter than going ahead.
And it would take more food to go on that far anyway."

"We have plenty of supplies we can share," Fritz said.

"And it makes sense to minimize your time alone."

"I guess I better call my friends, too. They might start looking for me." The words came out reluctantly. She called another number and left a message similar to the one for her mother.

They stood in silence for a while. Fritz seemed to be waiting for Kaimi to make some sort of decision.

"Do you really know how to find it?" Kaimi blurted. "I mean the trail. You don't even know where I came from."

Fritz laughed again. He had a sort of quiet chuckle that invited confidence. "I'm guessing you came from the South Slough Trailhead. It's the nearest one. And you were hiking from there to Devil's Rock."

"How did you figure that out?" Kaimi asked in surprise.

Fritz shrugged. "It's a popular route. Anyway, right here is where you got confused."

"Here?"

"Yup. Do you see where to go now?"

Kaimi looked up. There was a trail leading out of the clearing, and she pointed toward it. "I think that's where you and I came in."

"Nope. Look again."

She studied the tree line once more. "Oh, there's another trail going off that way. And another one. That might be one too," she said in wonder, rotating to look all around.

Fritz smiled at her bewilderment.

"There aren't any signs," Kaimi said, suddenly perturbed. "Someone should fix that."

"The markings are very old. People don't look carefully. Actually, there is a sign to the campsite."

Kaimi scanned the edges of the clearing once more. Finally, she saw a small board nailed to a tree with dark red letters. It was visible enough if you were watching where you were going. It read "The Valley." Her head was spinning and the fear closed in again. *Was that really the way they'd come here, the path she'd followed last night?*

"If you're staying with us for a while, let's head back," Fritz said, "It's almost lunchtime."

"Wait! Show me the main path now, the one to Devil's

Rock," she eked the words from a tight throat. "Please."

"Sure." He began walking the path that continued along the ridge, although it now began to slope slightly downhill. "If you look a short way down the various paths, there are reassurance markers. At least you won't go far out of your way if you pay attention. See, here's the main trail. This is the way back to South Slough. You were following yellow diamonds, right? "

"I... I think so," she stammered. "I was really just tagging along with the group."

"Hmmm. It's always a good idea for each hiker to understand the route," Fritz said. It might have sounded condescending, but somehow it didn't. He turned around and resumed walking. "So here's where you entered the clearing, and you veered to the right. That's how you found us. But if you veer left, you see the yellow trail continues."

They walked on, angling left, and soon there was one of the familiar yellow diamonds.

"Seems easy enough in the daylight," Kaimi admitted.

"The best plan is to have a map or guidebook," Fritz said. "I'm sure we have an extra map you can take with you when you decide which way to go. I can show you the other destinations on the map, too."

After lunch, Kaimi lay down in the sun for a nap. She couldn't believe how at peace she felt here. Fritz had been a perfect gentleman, not like most of the guys she knew. Michaela had eaten with her, and as they sat talking about trivial things, Kaimi had been overcome by such a safe and peaceful feeling that she had wanted to tell her new friend all about her father, and the dump of a trailer she shared with her mom. But she hadn't. It was as if Michaela already knew, but that was impossible.

Angela came and sat on the edge of the blanket that was spread in the sunshine. She brought a pile of cattail leaves, scissors and some sharpened sticks. She was working on another basket.

Kaimi thought maybe a child would be more honest with

her than an adult. "Where do you live when you aren't camping? Or is this your home all the time?" she asked.

Without looking up, as if the question was nothing startling, Angela answered, "This isn't our home. We have houses and I go to school, and the grown-ups have jobs. But that isn't really our home either."

"I don't understand."

"I don't either, really, but Mom and Dad say it's true."

Kaimi thought about that. The girl trusted her parents. There was nothing unusual about that. "What are you doing here? It doesn't look like just a camping trip."

Angela looked up. "Can you cut this end off? I can't hold the weaving in place and cut it at the same time."

After the end was snipped and tucked in, Angela looked Kaimi in the eyes. "We come here to pray and sing."

Kaimi tried to make her next question sound casual. "Who was that person who dove in the pool last night?"

She must have succeeded at sounding calm, because with no apparent alarm Angela pointed toward a thin figure, now wearing one of the robes, sawing a dead log into lengths of firewood. "He's over there. His name is Nathan.

"Why did he go in the water?"

"Oh, that's easy. He wanted to join our group. To be our friend, and to go to our real home with us when we leave."

"Angela!" someone called.

"That's my mom. Gotta go." The girl jumped up, gathered her partially finished basket and supplies, and skipped away.

Sounds a little weird. Maybe Nathan will talk to me. Kaimi stood, stretched, and walked cautiously toward the man Angela had pointed out.

"Hi, are you Nathan?"

The man straightened up and turned toward her. *He's old*, Kaimi realized, somehow shocked at this revelation. He didn't move like an older person.

"I am Nathan," he said. "You must be new."

"Yes, but how..."

Nathan laughed. "You don't have a robe."

"Oh!" Kaimi laughed too. "Do you mind if I ask you

something?"

"Fire away." Nathan leaned over to pick up a few logs, and then he stacked them neatly.

"Did you really join this group last night?"

The man shook his head. Wisps of thin gray hair shone in the sunlight. "Was it only last night? Seems like I've been here forever."

"But why did you want to become one of them? What made you want to do it," Kaimi suddenly cried, louder than she meant to. She looked around sheepishly to see if anyone had heard her.

"Let's sit down," Nathan invited. They sat side by side on the uncut portion of the log he'd been sawing.

She looked at his hands. The veins stood out. His fingers were gnarly with swollen knuckles and bent tips. The signs of advanced arthritis, Kaimi knew. Her grandmother's hands had looked this way. A wave of love, almost painful in its intensity washed over her as she thought of Gamma. And yet, Nathan had been working hard without complaining.

"Well," Nathan began to speak, and the vision of Gamma faded. "I couldn't see that I had anything to lose. I like it here. These people are the first ones to be kind to me in... a long time. I'd like to be that way to others."

There's a lot of sorrow behind those words. I can sense that, Kaimi thought. *And why do I feel everything so deeply, here in this valley?*

"But what do you know about them," she asked.

"Not everything," Nathan admitted.

"Doesn't that scare you?"

"Should it? I don't think we know everything about any of the people we choose to stay with. Certainly not our families. Not about someone we marry. We have to learn as we go."

"I never thought about it that way," Kaimi said.

Nathan chuckled. "It's not like I'm a prisoner or something. I'm staying because I want to."

"How did you get the robe? You had on shorts and a t-shirt."

"I don't really know. It was just there afterwards."

"After...?

"You know, after I took the plunge. Jumped in. Believed," Nathan said.

Believed. That was scary. Believed in what? Kaimi's mouth turned down, and her forehead puckered. She excused herself.

It was too much to take in. Kaimi crawled into her tent and zipped the front shut. She pulled the sleeping bag over her head.

But she couldn't sleep; that nap in the sun earlier had removed any possibility she could escape the questions through unconsciousness.

She went to find Muriel, the lady who had offered her a blanket. She didn't seem to be one of the people in charge, so maybe she wouldn't have an agenda. Kaimi didn't want to hear propaganda.

Muriel was sorting through a pan of berries, removing bugs and twigs. Kaimi sat down beside her.

"Hi," Muriel said.

"Hi yourself. Are those for dinner? How do you know those berries are safe to eat? I wouldn't have a clue."

"Michaela taught me." Muriel laughed. "You have to trust people, or you'd have to learn everything in the whole world for yourself."

True enough, but how do you know who to trust? Kaimi thought. Then she said, "Can I ask you something?

"Anything."

"How did you join this group? Did you dive in the pool, too?"

"I did. It seemed a really hard thing to do at the time, but now I can barely remember what I was like before then."

"Did you have to change? I mean, did you eat berries and live in the woods all your life?"

Muriel flipped her long brown hair away from her face. "Well, I guess I have changed, but I didn't have to before the pool. I came for a weekend trip with a friend and decided I wanted to belong. I'm a teacher most of the year."

"Oh! Elementary school?" Kaimi had thought about teaching, but she hadn't declared a major yet.

"Chemistry, actually. Junior college."

"Wow."

"But, how do I know I can trust any of you?" Kaimi asked.

"Well, that's a lot more serious question than which berries are safe." Muriel laid the pan aside and turned to look at Kaimi. Her eyes were soft and caring.

"Don't trust us. We're all here because we follow the guidebook. Nobody ever got lost using it. The one who wrote it knows the whole forest. We have faith in that one."

At dusk, as the last twilight faded, Kaimi stood on the flat rock at the end of the pool. She didn't understand it all, but she wanted to be caring and kind like these people. No one had ever treated her so well. No one here had even mentioned that she was chubby and plain. She wouldn't mind forgetting what her past life had been like.

Everyone else stood around the water, just like they had the night she came here. They began to hum and raise their arms. Kaimi lifted her arms too. The moonlight broke through the leafy canopy and all the arms reached for the sky. *Was that only yesterday?* But tonight she was looking at the moonlight from a different angle. Instead of a single ray, the light formed an oval portal, circling the pool.

It must just be the light reflecting on those white berries, but it looks like a door. It's now or never. Now.

Kaimi bent her knees and pushed off. As she entered the plane of the shining oval, she realized it was stretching, becoming three-dimensional and enveloping her like a cocoon, or a robe. High and ethereal music seemed to come from far away, maybe as far as the stars. A searing pain pierced her heart and she saw her mother and father. She saw them desperate for someone to care about them. She saw her friends, wandering without the guidebook.

***

He stumbled into the valley as dusk was fading into night.

PUBLISHED WORKS BY JOAN H. YOUNG

Non-Fiction:

North Country Cache: Adventures on a National Scenic Trail (2005 Independent Publishers, third place Regional Non-fiction)

Would You Dare?

Devotions for Hikers

Get Off the Couch with Joan

Fall Off the Couch Laughing

Midland to Mackinac Trail Guide

Fiction:
Anastasia Raven Mysteries

News from Dead Mule Swamp

The Hollow Tree at Dead Mule Swamp

Paddy Plays in Dead Mule Swamp

Bury the Hatchet in Dead Mule Swamp

Dead Mule Swamp Druggist

Dead Mule Swamp Mistletoe

Dubois Files Mysteries for Children

The Secret Cellar

The Hitchhiker

The ABZ Affair

The Bigg Boss

ABOUT THE AUTHOR

Joan H. Young has enjoyed the out-of-doors her entire life. Highlights of her outdoor adventures include Girl Scouting, which provided yearly training in camp skills, the opportunity to engage in a ten-day canoe trip, and numerous short backpacking excursions. She was selected to attend the 1965 Senior Scout Roundup in Coeur d'Alene, Idaho, an international event to which 10,000 girls were invited. She rode a bicycle from the Pacific to the Atlantic Ocean in 1986, and on August 3, 2010 became the first woman to complete the North Country National Scenic Trail on foot. Her mileage totaled 4395 miles. She often writes and gives media programs about her outdoor experiences.

In 2010 she began writing more fiction, including several award-winning short stories. *Accidentally Yours* collects many of these writings into one volume.

Visit booksleavingfootprints.com for more information.

www.ingramcontent.com/pod-product-compliance
Lightning Source LLC
Chambersburg PA
CBHW072233170626
46813CB00003B/1201